BOOK OF NO 3LEEP

無眠之书3

點子出版
IDEA PUBLICATION

不知道各位讀者過得怎樣呢?看過《無眠書》首兩集的讀者們,有否不期然地疑神疑鬼,又變得不敢相信別人呢?(還未看的,還不快點買來看?)

《無眠書》不經不覺來到第三集了,第一集分享過都市傳說、真實罪案,第二集講述人性醜惡,這次想抽離一點。

《無眠書 3 絕望夜》主要為讀者們以文字呈獻思想上的「恐怖」,這種恐怖遠比起能形象化的恐懼(例如:血腥不安的圖片、突襲的 Jump Scare、慘叫聲等等)更難表達,甚或無法解釋,可是前者帶來的影響卻深遠得多。

引用美國恐怖小說作家 Howard Phillips Lovecraft 的一句名言:「人類最古老而強烈的情緒,便是恐懼;而最古老最強烈的恐懼,便是對未知的恐懼。(The oldest and strongest emotion of mankind is fear, and the oldest and strongest kind of fear is fear of the unknown.)」

人類文明歷史雖然至少有一萬年,可是宇宙的年齡卻有約一百三十八億年。人類在宇宙當中,根本渺小得連一粒微塵也不如。人類未知的事情更有如銀河沙數,但正因為有著對未知題材的好奇，於是科學家費盡心神研究深不可測的宇宙，人們也幻想很多有關死後世界、時間旅行、外星生物等，創造了無窮無盡的異想作品。同樣地，要是人沒有這般的恐懼，也許就不會進步。

我們無法得知自己會否在下一秒死亡、世界會否末日，然而看過這本書的故事後，你可能會發現，原來無論你多麼努力也好，到頭來只會是徒然；又或是會豁然開朗，覺得已經沒有甚麼可以嚇怕自己了。

好了，現在就由我帶大家一同遊歷這場「絕望夜」，請你們懷著謙卑的心，探索詭秘的未知世界吧。

陳婉婷

CONTENTS
目 錄

別相信任何人 Trust No One

Thank you Kelly
謝謝你，Kelly 12

Message Deleted
訊息已刪除 16

Uncle Tommy's Visit
Tommy 叔叔的探訪 19

Keeping Up with the Joneses
人民慶典 22

Sister Sister
姊妹情深 24

I Trusted Her
她背叛我 27

The Cleaner
清潔工的辛酸 29

I'm Not Sure I Want to Know
我不想知道 32

My Last Time Babysitting
最後一次當保姆 34

He Took Me to the Lake
他帶我到湖邊 37

Daisy
雛菊 39

If You Hear a Child Crying Alone
at Night, Run
別理會叢林裏的求救聲 41

Stranger Danger
生人勿近 43

別掉以輕心 Stay Alert

Your Face Gives It Away
相由心生 47

Give Me a Smile
笑一個吧 49

Father
神父 52

There, there...
喝吧喝吧 55

Naomi Losing Teeth
牙仙子傳說 56

Twenty Years in the Dark
被困黑暗二十年 59

The End of the Hallway
長廊的盡頭 61

The Sheriff's Announcement
警長的聲明 63

What are Monsters, Really?
怎樣才算是怪物？ 66

The Basement
流浪貓 68

The Dark Night
黑夜降臨 70

The Year They Banned Porn
色情片被禁以後 73

別自以為是
Be Modest and Humble

It's a Horrible Life
悲劇人生 78

Dances With Sixteen Devils
與十六位惡魔共舞 81

Gaslight
假面人 85

Life of a Traitor
叛徒的餘生 88

My Girlfriend was Always Afraid
of Being Alone
長伴身旁 91

5070
5070 立方英吋 92

The Thing About Lake Emily
艾米麗湖的秘密 95

A Twin Thing
雙胞胎才懂的事 98

The Gatekeeper
看門人 100

The Alcoholic
酒鬼 102

Nobody's Perfect
無人完美 106

I Have Seven Minutes Before I Die
死前七分鐘 108

Just 60 Seconds
只得六十秒 111

別低估人性 Value Humanity

I Got a Sound Wave Tattoo,
But the Audio Came Out Wrong
聲軌紋身 116

There's a Child Abuser in My Home
兒童虐待案 118

Smith & Wesson
槍櫃 121

I Witnessed Everything Over Skype
我在 Skype 目睹了一切 123

I Believe in You
堅定的信心 126

The Red Water Lily
紅睡蓮 128

Monsters Beneath the Surface
藏在底下的怪物 131

Everything to Lose
破釜沉舟 134

A Cure for Depression
抑鬱症治療 137

That Day Had Teeth
淡黃的一天 140

The Pointing Girl
指劃女孩 143

The Sting Still Hurt
蛇蠍心腸 146

I Reported a Missing Person
匯報失蹤人口 149

別小看世界 Respect the World

This is What You Get
When You Mess With Us
罪有應得 154

The Race Goes On Forever
永無止境的比賽 157

Losing at Poker to a Demon
惡魔的玩笑 159

A Time to Be Born, a Time to Die
生有時，死有時 162

While, not For
榮休之喜 165

There's No Reason to Be Afraid
善良的鬼魂 168

Regrets
後悔 170

Breaking Amy
壞心的哥哥 171

Where Were You When Time Froze?
時間靜止當刻你在幹甚麼？.......174

Get Me Away from Here, I'm Dying
厭倦了乏味的生活.................177

Wish Upon a Star
向流星許願 180

To Be Young and Healthy Again
青春常駐，身體健康..............182

I Have to Live Every Day Twice
預習生活...........................185

Trust No One
別 相 信 任 何 人

Thank You Kelly

"...Please...h-h-hurry..."

"Sir, we have your location and the emergency services are on their way."

"...Hurry...s-s-six..."

"I'm sorry sir your breathing is very heavy and you're still mumbling slightly, I can't hear you very well. Could you speak up please?"

"...S-s-s..."

"I...I need you to stay on the line for me, okay? ...Can you do that?"

"...yesss..."

"Okay, good, good. Like I just said, the emergency services are on their way and will be with you in the next few minutes. I'm going to stay on the phone with you until they get there, okay?"

"...."

"What's your name, sir?"

"..."

"Sir? Are you there?"

"...yes."

謝謝你，Kelly

「……拜託……快、快、快點……」

「先生，我們已得悉你的所在位置，救援人員亦正趕至現場。」

「……快點……六、六、六……」

「不好意思，先生，你的喘氣聲太大了，而且説話有點含糊，我聽得不太清楚，你可以説大聲一點嗎？」

「……呼、呼、呼……」

「你……你不要掛線，好嗎？……你能做到嗎？」

「……好……的……」

「好的，非常好。就如我剛才所説，救援人員正趕至現場，幾分鐘內便會來到救你。在他們到達之前，我都會一直跟你通話，明白嗎？」

「……」

「先生，你叫甚麼名字？」

「……」

「先生？你在嗎？」

「……在。」

"...Sir, my name is Kelly, and I'm here to help you. Could you tell me your name?"

"...s-sick."
"Say again please?"

"...S-Six."
"Are you saying, six? As in the number six?"

"...bo...bo....six..."
"Sir?"

"...six...bo..."
"Sir? Stay with me, okay? They'll be there any moment now...sir?....Hello?!"

"..."

"195, this is control, come in."
"...195, go ahead."

"195 Please be advised there's a possibility of bodies at the scene. What's your ETA?"

「……先生，我的名字是 Kelly，我是來幫助你的。你能告訴我你的名字嗎？」

「……六、陸。」
「請你再說一遍好嗎？」

「……六、六。」
「你是説六嗎？數目字的六嗎？」

「……**彈**……**彈**……**六**……」
「先生？」

「……六……**彈**……」
「先生？堅持住！好嗎？他們很快就到了……先生？……喂喂？！」

「……」

「*195，這是控制室，請接線。*」
「*……這是 195，請説。*」

「*195 請注意，現場可能有屍體。你們預計甚麼時候到達？*」

"...45 seconds."

"The line is still open but we seem to have lost contact with the caller, proceed with caution, incident still unknown."

"...195 copy that."

"Sir? This is Kelly again. Can you still hear me?"

"..."

"If you can, they will be with you any second now, okay?"

"...okay...good...open..."

"...Sir?"

"...open..."

"Control, this is 195, we are now at the scene, proceeding through both front and rear entrances."

Kelly's eyes unknowingly glanced over the time, and her mind finally clicked...5:59...6:00...

"195 this is control, do not enter the property! I repeat, do not enter the prop..."

「……四十五秒後。」

「電話仍在接通狀態，但我們似乎已經與致電者失去聯繫，尚未了解案件類型，請謹慎行事。」

「……195 收到。」

「先生？我是 Kelly，我回來了。你聽得到我講話嗎？」

「……」

「如果你聽到的話，我跟你說喔，他們很快就會來救你了，知道了嗎？」

「……好吧……好……開……」

「……先生？」

「……打開……」

「控制室，這是 195，我們現在到了現場，準備在前門和後門一起進去。」

Kelly 不經意地瞥了時鐘一眼，五點五十九分、六點正……她終於想通了……

「195，這是控制室，不要進去！我重複，不要進……」

The explosion rapidly increased in volume through the airwaves. The extreme release of energy completely tore the building apart, killing anyone within 25 feet of the blast zone.

The police force lost 15 officers in that moment, the ambulance lost 6 and the fire service lost 12. The neighbours house was also half blown apart, taking both the bedroom and the life of a three year old girl.

The line was still open and heavy breathing could clearly be heard. The last thing she expected to hear next, was laughter.

"...Ha ha haaa...ha ha ha haaa....ahhh.....thank you, Kelly. That was fun to watch..."

The line finally went dead.

話筒突然傳來了爆炸巨響。爆炸釋放出極大的能量，粉碎了建築物，而且把爆炸方圓二十五英尺範圍內的所有人都殺光了。

那一瞬間，造成了十五名警察、六名救護人員、十二名消防員殉職。鄰近的房子也被炸了一半，把睡房連同房內一名三歲女孩的性命一同毀掉了。

電話仍在接通狀態，話筒裏可以清楚聽見沉重的呼吸聲。她早就料到，接下來聽到的，會是笑聲。

「……哈哈哈……哈哈哈哈……啊……謝謝你呢，Kelly，我看得很開心……」

電話終於掛線了。

Message Deleted

"You-have-nine-new-messages, message-one;"
"Hi, this is a message for Miss Jenna Crawfield, my name's Elaine and I'm calling from Look-Forward-Security, this call is regarding..."

"Message-deleted, message-two;"
"Hey babe, I'm running an hour late, got held up in a meeting, so I'll just see you at the party, okay. Love you, bye."

"Message-deleted, message-three;"
"Jen, its me pick up...C'mon, babe, don't be like this. I said I was sorry... Jen?...pick up, come on...Jen?...argh."

"Message-deleted, Message-four;"
"Jenna, please just talk to me... please?... At least let me fully explain to you what happened with her...Jen?... Come on please, I don't want to do this over the phone... if you don't pick up in the next five seconds, I'm coming over ... ... right I'm coming over."

"Message-deleted, message-five;"
"So you think keying the words tiny limp dick on my car is funny, do ya!? You fucking cunt! Jen, I swear to god, the next time I see you, I'm gonna slice open your neck with these same car keys, and ram the whole damn set down your fucking whore throat! Aarrgh! Fuck you, Jen, fuck you!"

訊息已刪除

「你有九個新訊息，第一個訊息；」
「你好，這是給 Jenna Crawfield 小姐的訊息，我是代表期待保安公司的 Elaine，打電話過來是有關⋯⋯」

「訊息已刪除，第二個訊息；」
「寶貝，我會遲一個小時才到啊，剛剛要開會，我們待會直接在派對碰面吧，好吧，愛你，再見。」

「訊息已刪除，第三個訊息；」
「Jen，是我啊，接電話吧。來嘛寶貝，不要這樣嘛。我已經跟你道歉了啊 Jen⋯⋯接電話嘛，好嗎 Jen？⋯⋯唉啊。」

「訊息已刪除，第四個訊息：」
「Jenna，拜託你聽電話好嗎？至少讓我解釋一下跟她的事好嗎，Jen？來吧，拜託你了，我不想在電話裏談這件事啊。如果你五秒之內還不接電話的話，我就過來找你⋯⋯⋯⋯⋯⋯⋯⋯⋯⋯⋯⋯⋯⋯好吧，我過來找你。」

「訊息已刪除，第五個訊息；」
「你覺得用鑰匙在我的車子劃上『又小又軟的雞雞』很好玩嗎？你這個他媽的臭婊子。Jen，我向天發誓，下次見到你時，我會用同一把車匙，割開你的脖子，再把整串鑰匙塞進你這個臭三八的喉嚨裏！啊！！！去你的，Jen，去你的！」

"Message-deleted, message-six;"

"Jenna, this is your mother... I know its been a long time since we last spoke and er... well, this isn't going to be easy to say whether we had still been in touch or not, but er... you're father has just died. He was...He was murdered, Jenna...Everyone at his precinct are on the case. Captain Anderson has assured me..."

"Message-deleted, message-seven;"

"...I can see you Jen...yep! I can see you right now.... You think I won't be able to get in, don't you? You think this little, shitty, prehistoric, Look-Forward-Security camera, which looks already broken, is going to stop me?... You think you're soo safe because of Daddy...Well....You're not the only one who has family in the right places, Jen..."

"Message-deleted, message-eight;"

"Baby...baby I'm so sorry... I never should've...I never should've done any of this stuff. I just wanted you to talk to me again and, and, and listen to me again...I Never meant for this to happen, I never meant for him to kill..."

"Message-deleted, message-nine;"

"I hope someone is hearing this message, my father is a murderer and must be stopped...He has killed two people tonight...His name is Jack An..."

「訊息已刪除，第六個訊息；」

「Jenna，是媽媽打來啊。我知道我們已經很久沒有聊天了，呃……是這樣的，無論我們一直以來有沒有聯絡也好，這件事都很難說出口，可是呃……你爸爸過世了。他……他是被殺的。每位隸屬他警區的探員都在密切關注他的案件。Anderson隊長向我保證……」

「訊息已刪除，第七個訊息；」

「……我看到你了喔Jen！我真的看到你了啊……你以為我無法進來對嗎？你以為期待保安那個又小又沒用的史前攝錄機能阻止我嗎？更不用說它看起來早已壞掉啦。你以為自己有父親撐腰就很安全了嗎？哼，不是只有你一個才能靠家人的關係啊，Jen……」

「訊息已刪除，第八個訊息；」

「寶貝……寶貝對不起……我不應該……絕對不應該做這回事。我只是想你再跟我說說話，還有，還有再聽我解釋而已……我沒有想過會發生這種事，也沒有想過他會殺了……」

「訊息已刪除，第九個訊息；」

「我希望有人會聽到這個訊息，我父親是個殺人犯，你們必須制止他……他今晚殺了兩個人……他的名字是Jack An……」

"Message-deleted, end-of-messages."

The crime scene was quickly filling with a variety of government agencies.

Sergeant: "Did you find anything on the answering machine?"
Captain Anderson: "No, nothing. It was clean."

「訊息已刪除，再沒有新訊息。」

案發現場迅速聚滿了不同政府機構的人員。

警長：「錄音電話裏頭有甚麼發現嗎？」
Anderson 隊長：「沒有，甚麼都沒有，裏面是空的。」

Uncle Tommy's Visit

"Now remember, I don't want you talking to him unless I'm around, you hear?"

"Yes, dad."

"I'm serious. Now tuck in your shirt—he's here."

The front door swung open and there stood Uncle Tommy, drenched in sweat from a day's work in the summer heat.

"It's a scorcher out there, ain't it?" he said, putting his bag on the floor and untying his boots. "I appreciate you letting me crash for the night."

"Just so long as you're gone in the morning," my dad replied coldly.

"Of course."

"Now," Uncle Tommy said, turning to me and lowering himself to a knee. "Where's my hug at? Been a while since I seen you last."

I took a couple steps toward him and leaned in for a hug. His tight embrace made me uncomfortable, and I let out a light whimper.

"Don't you know it's a hundred degrees out there?" **he asked, tugging at my long sleeves.**

"I haven't been outside today," I recited to him.

Tommy叔叔的探訪

「給我記好了，要是我不在的話，你不可以跟他說話，聽到了嗎？」

「知道了，爸爸。」

「我是認真的，快點把襯衫披好，他來了。」

前門打開了，在炎夏中工作了一整天、汗流浹背的 Tommy 叔叔就站在那裏。

「哎呀，快要熱死人了！」他把袋子放在地上後，邊解開靴子的鞋帶邊說：「很感激你讓我借宿一宵。」

「只要你天光時離開就好了。」爸爸冷冷地道。

「沒問題。」

「好了。」Tommy 叔叔轉過來單膝跪在我前面，「快來給我一個擁抱，好一陣子沒有看見你了呢！」

我向他走前了幾步，然後給他一個擁抱。Tommy 叔叔把我抱得太緊了，讓我有點不舒服，不禁悶哼了一聲。

「你不知道今天外面快三十八度了嗎？」他邊問邊用力拉扯我的長袖子。

「我今天沒有出門。」我把答案背誦出來。

"Don't you have some chores to finish up?" Dad interjected.

I knew that was my cue to leave, so I shuffled off to my room.

Later that night I lay in bed. I tossed and turned, unable to be comfortable, when I heard the thud of footsteps in the hallway outside my bedroom. After several long seconds of silence, the door opened quietly, the dark silhouette of a man entered the room, and the door closed again. For several more seconds there was nothing but unrelenting silence. I might have thought I had dreamt it all if it weren't for the sound of a hushed breath being carefully released.

I could feel him getting nearer. The warmth of another person in the room was unfamiliar at this hour.

I was not prepared for this; I prayed he would go away, to even come back in the morning if he must.

He reached down and touched me. He rolled me onto my stomach and lifted up my shirt. From the corner of my eye I could see two things: the faint beam of a pocket flashlight, and Uncle Tommy's eyes studying my bare skin. His rough fingers ran up and down my back. Suddenly, he got up and walked to the bedroom door and left. I tried again to fall asleep, eventually succeeding.

「你不是還有事要做嗎？」爸爸插話道。

我知道那是提醒我離開的說話，所以我轉身回到自己房間。

當晚我躺在床上，聽見房門外的走廊傳出了腳步聲，我輾轉反側，怎樣也覺得不舒服。片刻的寂靜後，房門悄悄地打開了，一個男子的黑影走了進來，門就關上了，然後又再安靜了好一陣子。要不是本來屏息的他呼了一口氣，我還以為自己只是在做夢。

我感覺到他逐漸靠近，這個時間有另一個人的溫暖氣息在我房間出現，這種感覺很陌生。

我還沒有做好準備，我祈禱希望他會走開，或者他一定要來的話，也拜託在白天才來吧⋯⋯

他俯身向我，然後觸摸我。他把我的被子扯到肚子位置，接著把我的上衣掀起。我從眼角瞥到兩樣東西：從袖珍手電筒發出的微弱光線，和 Tommy 叔叔專注研究我皮膚的雙眼。他粗糙的手指向上摸，又向下摸我的背。他突然站起來走向房門離開了。我再次嘗試入睡，最後也順利睡著了。

He was gone by the time I awoke.

Around noon the phone rang while my father was out.

"Hello?" I answered.
"Hey buddy."

"Uncle Tommy?"
"Yeah. Your dad around?"

"No sir. Went to the store."
"Good," he said, sounding a bit nervous. He paused for a moment. "I'm calling about last night. I don't know if you were awake or not—"

"I was."
"Well, then I'll just get right to it. I've got a question for you, and I need for you to be honest with me. Can you do that?"

"Yes, sir."
"How'd you get all them bruises?"

我醒來時 Tommy 叔叔已經走了。

大約中午時分，爸爸到外面去了的時候，電話響起了。

「你好。」我接了電話。
「嘿，小伙子。」

「Tommy 叔叔？」
「是的，你爸爸在嗎？」

「不在啊叔叔，他到商店去了。」
「很好。」他的聲線聽起來有點緊張，「我打過來是想跟你說說昨晚的事，我不知道你當時有沒有醒過來⋯⋯」

「我是清醒的。」
「那麼，我就直接說了。我想問你一個問題，你要對我說實話，可以嗎？」

「好的，叔叔。」
「那些瘀傷是怎麼一回事？」

Keeping Up with the Joneses

Sadie's parents were fighting again.

"This is just so typical of you," said her mom, her voice breaking. "You never follow through on anything. You said we'd go together, as a family. You promised."

Sadie knew they were arguing about the Town Festival. If they didn't go soon, they'd miss it. The whole town was probably already there. Sadie imagined them dancing, and enjoying cake and punch and candy and all the other things she normally wasn't allowed. It was so unfair.

Her father said something Sadie couldn't hear. His voice was low and calm, which meant he was very, very angry.

"I won't let you!" her mom screamed, and then, "Sadie! Hide!"

There was a loud crash. Sadie heard her father moving from room to room, calling her name. She squeezed herself behind a dresser.

Her father wasn't always scary. Just a few nights ago they'd sat together in the yard, looking at the sky. He'd shown her the constellations, and explained how the positions of the planets and stars determined the date of the Town Festival.

人民慶典

Sadie 的父母又在吵架了。

「你總是這個老樣子!」Sadie 母親聲音沙啞地說著,「你永遠都只懂半途而廢。你說過我們會一起去的,一家人整整齊齊地去的。你答應過我的啊!」

Sadie 知道他們正為小鎮的慶典爭論著。如果他們還不快點出門,就趕不及參與慶典了。整個小鎮的市民可能都已經到了那裏。Sadie 想像著大家在跳舞、吃著美味的蛋糕、果汁和糖果,還做著一些父母平常不允許自己做的其他事情。這樣太不公平了。

Sadie 父親說了些甚麼,可是她聽不見。父親的聲音低沉而平靜,這意味著他非常生氣,怒不可遏。

「我不會讓你這樣做的!」她母親尖叫著,然後嚷道:「Sadie!躲起來!」

接著傳來了一聲巨響。Sadie 聽見父親邊從各個房間走動著,邊叫喊著她的名字。她擠到了梳妝枱後面躲著。

父親不是經常這般可怕的。就在幾天前的一個晚上,Sadie 跟父親一起坐在院子裏,看著天空。父親向她展示著各個星

Behind the dresser, Sadie began to cry. It seemed like hours passed. Then she heard a scuffle down the hallway, and the front door slamming shut. In the silence that followed, Sadie crawled out of her hiding place and peeked out the window.

The Festival was over. She'd missed everything. There had definitely been dancing; Sadie could tell because everyone was tired out, sleeping face-down, right on the ground. They'd obviously had punch too; **she could see paper cups scattered everywhere, some of them still half-full of a purple-colored drink.**

Sadie's mom came into the room and sat on the bed.

"It's safe now, baby," she said. "He's gone."
"But we missed the Festival."

Her mom nodded. "I know, baby, but don't be sad. We still get to have punch."

She handed Sadie a paper cup filled with purple liquid, so sweet it tasted just like heaven.

座，又解釋了行星和恆星的位置，將如何決定慶典的日期。

躲在梳妝枱後面的 Sadie 哭泣起來。時間過得很慢，好像已經過了幾個小時般難熬。然後她聽見走廊裏傳出扭打聲，接著是前門砰的關門聲。在隨後的一片沉默中，Sadie 從梳妝枱後爬了出來，往窗外窺看著。

慶典結束了。她錯過了這一切。剛剛大家肯定都在跳舞——Sadie 看得出來，因為每個人都累透了，面朝下的趴在地上睡著了。大家也顯然喝過了果汁——**她看見紙杯散落一地，其中一些還盛著半滿的紫色飲料。**

Sadie 母親走進了房間，坐到床上。

「現在安全了，寶貝……」她說：「他走了。」
「可是我們已經錯過慶典了啊。」

她母親點了點頭：「我知道，寶貝，但請不要傷心。我們還是會喝果汁的呢。」

她把一個紙杯遞了給 Sadie，杯裏裝滿紫色的液體，很甜，喝起來就像天堂一樣。

Sister Sister

When I was ten, my best friend Amy had a little sister, Tessa, who disappeared. Late one night their mom felt a draft in the house, and when she went downstairs to investigate, she found the front door wide open. Tessa was gone. There were no clues, no evidence. The girl had vanished.

Initially there was talk of abduction, but the family kept their house locked, and the girls didn't open doors for strangers. Police found no sign of a break-in or struggle.

Tessa was the kind of kid who saved animals: baby birds, turtles, deer, whatever. **She was always hearing some poor injured creature's cries** and following them into the woods that surrounded the house. So everyone thought she'd just ventured outside on her own and had gotten lost.

When months passed with no real progress on the case, Amy's parents went missing too, but in a different way. They drank too much and slept incessantly, crippled by guilt and misery. Amy rarely saw them.

It was some fishermen who finally found Tessa, a few miles down the river. It wasn't easy to identify her body, and even after the autopsy nobody was sure what had happened to her.

姊妹情深

我十歲時，好朋友 Amy 的妹妹 Tessa 失蹤了。那天晚上，Amy 的媽媽感到房子裏有股冷空氣吹過，下樓查看發生甚麼事時，她發現前門敞開著，而 Tessa 不見了。找不著任何線索或證據。Tessa 就這樣憑空消失了。

最初大家都懷疑 Tessa 是被綁架，但他們一家習慣把房子鎖起來，兩個女兒也不會開門給陌生人。警方也沒有發現任何強行闖入或打鬥的跡象。

Tessa 是個很有愛心的孩子，樂於拯救動物，例如幼鳥、烏龜、鹿等等。**她總能聽到一些受傷動物發出的悲鳴聲**，然後她便會隨著聲音走進她家周圍的樹林裏。所以大家都認為她只是獨自在外面冒險之後迷路了。

幾個月過去了，案件仍然沒有甚麼進展，Amy 的父母也以另一種方式消失不見了。他們常常都會喝得酩酊大醉，又不分晝夜地睡覺，被內疚和悲痛困住了自己。所以 Amy 很少見到他們。

終於有一天，一些漁民在沿著河流下游幾英里的地方找到了 Tessa。她的屍體已經變得很難辨認了，即使法醫替她驗屍後，也沒有人能肯定她到底因為甚麼事而死亡。

"Well, at least now they have closure," everyone said.

Amy didn't see it that way.

She called me shortly after the funeral, sobbing and choking on her breath.

"I think Tessa's still alive," she said. "I heard her crying last night, outside in the woods. Nobody believes me."

I believed her, but I didn't think it was Tessa. I thought it was her ghost.

I agreed to sleep over at Amy's house that night. I brought my dog along for protection, and Amy and I fell asleep with our fingers tangled in his warm fur. Something woke us up a few hours later.

There was a voice outside, faint, the words indecipherable, but it was definitely Tessa. My hands shook as I pulled on my shoes. I wasn't ready to see a ghost.

「那麼，至少現在他們算是得到解脫了吧。」大家都這樣說。

Amy 卻不這麼認為。

她在葬禮後不久打了電話給我，那時她哭得快要窒息了。

「我覺得 Tessa 還是活著的。」她說：「我昨晚聽見她在樹林裏哭泣，可是沒有人相信我。」

我相信她，但我不認為那是真的 Tessa，我覺得那只是她的鬼魂。

我答應了 Amy 那天晚上到她家過夜。我帶上了我的狗，希望牠能保護我們。我和 Amy 摸著牠，我們的手指還纏在牠溫暖的毛上，不知不覺便睡著了。幾個小時後，有些東西把我們弄醒了。

外面傳來了一把微弱的聲音，雖然聽不清楚她在說甚麼，但那肯定是 Tessa 的聲音。穿鞋子時我的雙手不禁顫抖，我還沒有準備好要看見鬼魂呢⋯⋯

As soon as Amy opened the door, my dog burst out of the house, barking like a maniac. We had no choice but to follow him into the woods. We searched around for a while, but there was no sign of Tessa.

"Your dumb dog chased her away," said Amy, tears running down her face. She fled toward the house. As I turned to follow her, I tripped on something.

It was a duffle bag. I forced myself to look inside. Duct tape. Plastic zip-tie handcuffs. A knife.

And a tape recorder.

When I pushed the "play" button, I heard Tessa's voice, crying and screaming for Amy to save her, and begging someone to let her go.

Amy 一打開門，我的狗就馬上衝了出去，瘋狂吠個不停。我們別無選擇，只好跟著牠走進樹林。我們搜索了一會兒，可是哪裏都找不著 Tessa 的蹤影。

「你的笨狗趕走了她！」Amy 説道，淚珠順著臉蛋滾滾落下。説罷她便向房子的方向跑走了。當我轉身追她時，我絆倒了些甚麼。

是一個行李袋。我迫自己看看裏面有甚麼東西：一綑牛皮膠帶、一堆塑膠索帶手銬、一把刀。

還有一部錄音機。

當我按下播放鍵時，我聽見 Tessa 的聲音，她一邊大聲哭喊著叫 Amy 來拯救她，一邊乞求某人讓她離開。

I Trusted Her

"I'm leaving and I'm taking the kids."

I re-read the message for what seemed like the hundredth time today.

I've been married to this woman for almost 6 years, dated her for even longer. But still she does this to me!

I trusted her with the kids. Trusted her to look after them while I worked. But I guess it was too much to ask.

And now, after this message, I can see my future darken.

I had a plan, see? There was a way out of this poverty. **The kids were our way out. They were supposed to secure our future.** And now, she's taken them from me.

I unlock the door to an empty house.

But still I hope. Still I think she might have changed her mind and stayed.

I rush through the house checking every room in the house. I check the bedroom for her. I check the bathroom. I check the basement.

她背叛我

「我要走了，還有，我把孩子們一起帶走了。」

我重複讀著這個短訊，仿佛已是今天的一百遍。

我和她結婚六年了，交往的時間更是長久，可是她竟然這樣對我！

我相信她，所以才會在工作時把孩子交給她照顧，不過對她來說可能是個過分的要求吧。

但當我看到那個短訊之後，我的未來就像被陰霾籠罩了。

明明我有計劃，我想了個方法讓我們脫貧、改善生活啊？**孩子們就是我們的希望，他們理應是保障我們未來的投資才對啊**？可是現在，她卻擅自帶走了孩子們。

插進鑰匙、扭開門把後，屋子裏空無一人。

我還在奢想，她會回心轉意留下來。

我在屋子裏東奔西跑，查看每個房間；睡房、浴室、地下室，我統統都找過了。

Nothing. Empty.

Well, I guess this is the end.

As I sit on the couch drinking my third glass of whiskey, I can hear the sirens approaching.

I never should have trusted her with the hostages.

甚麼都沒有，只有一片空蕩蕩。

好吧，我想一切就這樣完了吧。

坐在沙發上喝著第三杯威士忌的我，聽見警笛聲逐漸接近。

我早就不該讓她看管那些人質。

The Cleaner

One summer, I worked as a house cleaner for this family down the road for some pocket money. It was fun, mostly.

"Hello, is anybody home?", I called, out of habit, as I poked my head through the door.

"Yes, we are upstairs", answered the husband. "Please go ahead and just ignore us."

OK, cool! As I said, this was a fun, simple job, so I went ahead. **I heard the door being shut upstairs, some rhythmic pounding noises,** and then, alas, some moaning.

"Reeeally?!", I sighed exaggeratedly and muttered to myself. "You know I'm down here, riiiiight?!"

Putting on my headphones, I shook my head in disgust one more time, before continuing with the work, pretending that I knew nothing.

It was a while before I heard some loud footsteps running down the hollow timber stairs, the sound of the front door flung open, then slammed shut, and finally, the sound of the lock clicked. "Probably the husband going somewhere", I shrugged.

清潔工的辛酸

為了賺零用錢，有一年夏天，我到了馬路邊這個家庭當臨時清潔工。這份工作大部分時間都很有趣。

「你好，請問有人在家嗎？」我把頭伸進門口，習慣性地大聲問道。

「有啊，我們在樓上。」先生回答：「請自便吧，你不用管我們。」

好的，太棒了！正如我所說，這是個有趣又簡單的工作，所以我進了房子開始清潔。**我聽到樓上傳來關門聲，然後是一些有節奏的砰砰響聲，接著，唉，是一些呻吟聲。**

「真的假的？！」我誇張地嘆了口氣，喃喃自語道：「你們知道我在這裏的，對——吧——？！」

戴上耳機的我，再次厭惡地搖了搖頭，然後繼續工作，假裝甚麼都不知道。

過了一會兒，我才聽到一些響亮的腳步聲，在空心的木樓梯上奔跑，前門打開，然後砰地關上，最後是上鎖的聲音。可能是先生趕著要去某個地方吧，我心想，聳了聳肩。

Half an hour later, finished with the work downstairs, I gathered all the stuff and headed upstairs. Their bedroom door was still closed, and no sound was emanating from it.

"Well this is convenient isn't it, how am I supposed to hoover the house now Mrs. I-Will-Sleep-Whenever-I-Want?", I thought bitterly. "I don't have all day to stand here waiting for you to wake up!"

Faced with no other choice, I had to knock on the door. "Excuse me, are you sleeping in there? Can I hoover the house?"

No answer, but the door slowly drifted open. It wasn't locked.

I screamed out in horror when the scene in the bedroom raped my vision. Red, the whole bed was red with blood. The wife lay dead in the middle, a knife sticking out of her chest. Her head turned to the door and her unblinking eyes stared directly into mine.

I reacted like the idiot that I was, ran up to her corpse and shook her, like that would make a difference.

"Hey, wake up, can you hear me, wake up. Hey..."

半小時後，我完成了樓下的清潔工作，我收拾好所有東西，然後向樓上進發。他們的臥室門仍然關閉，現在已經沒有聲音了。

「哇，這真是很方便呢！我現在應該怎麼樣把你的房子清潔乾淨呢，這位『我要睡就睡』太太？」我憤怨地想著，「老子可不會花一整天站在這裏等著你醒來啊！」

別無選擇的我，只好敲門。「不好意思，請問你正在睡覺嗎？我可以用吸塵機嗎？」

沒有回應，可是門慢慢地打開了。門沒有鎖。

當睡房裏的場景入侵了我的視線時，我驚恐地尖叫著。一片血紅，整張床滿是染血的紅色。太太躺在了床中央，胸口插著一把刀。她的臉面向房間門口，目不轉睛的直視著我。

我作出白痴般的反應——跑到她的屍體旁並搖晃她，以為可以扭轉乾坤。

「喂，醒醒吧，你能聽見嗎？醒來啊。喂……」

The congealed blood on her chest stuck on my cleaning gloves, but I did not give up. I continued to shake and call, until the sound of sirens swamped into my ears.

I heard hurried footsteps and muffled voices. Then one, louder than the rest - it was the husband's voice.

"Please hurry up! I locked the murderer inside!"

縱然太太傷口上凝結了的血液，黏滿了清潔手套，我仍然沒有放棄。我繼續邊搖晃她邊叫喊著，直到警笛聲湧進我的耳朵。

接下來我聽見匆匆的腳步聲和很多低沉的說話聲。當中有一把聲音，比其他人更響亮──那是先生的聲音。

「請你們快點！我把兇手鎖了在裏面！」

I'm Not Sure I Want to Know

"You wanna know what your mistake was?"

I sat in the back of the squad car, doing my best to look bored, unaffected. In reality, my mind was racing. It wasn't that I thought I'd never be caught. It was just that I didn't think it would be so soon. I'd only gotten two – a brunette and a redhead – and I'd been careful not to leave any traces at the scenes. I was certain I was in the clear.

Until two days after I finished with the redhead, and Officer Asshole came knocking on my door.

"See, it wasn't that you nicked your finger and left blood at the scene. No, you could've come back from that."

I tested my handcuffs, even though I knew it wouldn't do any good. Even if I got them off, I couldn't get out of the back of the car. I was well and truly fucked.

"And it wasn't the fact that you left the murder weapon behind. No fingerprints on it, so that wouldn't have helped us much anyway."

I should have had a plan for this, but I didn't. I'd need an attorney, but I'm not stupid – I knew I was in deep shit. My best-case scenario was probably life in prison. I wasn't ready

我不想知道

「你想知道自己犯了甚麼錯誤嗎？」

我坐在警車的後座，盡力讓自己看起來很無聊，而且不受影響。事實上，我的腦袋飛快地狂轉著。不是因為我以為自己永遠不會被抓到，而是我沒想過會這麼快就被抓了。我只搞定了兩個：一個黑髮女郎和一個紅髮女郎，我一直以來都很小心，不會在現場留下任何痕跡。那時我很肯定自己沒有任何破綻。

直到我搞定紅髮的兩天後，有個混蛋警察來敲我的門。

「你並非錯在割傷了手指上並留下血跡。不是的，因為你大可以回來把血跡處理掉。」

我試著掙脫手銬，儘管我知道這一點屁用都沒有。即使我解開了手銬也好，我也無法從車子的後方逃脫。我徹頭徹尾地完蛋了。

「你也不是錯在遺下了兇器，而且它上面沒有指紋，所以就算我們得到這個證物也好，對破案並沒有甚麼大幫助。」

我早該想到這個狀況，然後想出相應的逃脫計劃，可是我並沒有想過。我需要一位律師，但我不是傻子——我知道自己

to think worst-case just yet.

"No, for how much of a… mess you left when you murdered Bernadette, you did a pretty good job, I'll give you that much. But you screwed up."

Bernadette, huh? Pretty name. I watched as the cop switched lanes and started to slow down. We were still a good ten miles from town.

He made eye contact with me in the rearview mirror and smiled.

"Your mistake, you see…"

He paused as he turned off the main highway onto a small gravel road nearly hidden by the trees. When he looked at me again, the smile was gone and his eyes were cold.

"…was believing that I'm really a cop."

麻煩大了。對我而言，最好的情況可能是在獄中度過餘生。然而最糟糕的情況……我還沒準備好去想呢。

「不是的，你在謀殺 Bernadette 時留下的麻煩事……並不多，你處理得不錯，我是說真的啊。但你犯了一個大錯。」

Bernadette，**對吧？名字很好聽**。我看著警察轉換了車道並開始減速。我們距離城鎮還有十英里遠。

他微笑著，在倒後鏡中與我四目交投。

「你錯在……」

他頓了頓，把車子駛離主幹道，然後走進一條幾乎被樹木完全遮蔽的碎石路上。當他再次看著我時，笑容消失了，眼裏只得冷漠。

「……相信我真的是個警察。」

My Last Time Babysitting

I checked my watch as I walked up to the door. Ten minutes late. I had been babysitting for them for six months, I was sure they wouldn't mind.

Mr. Lopez answered the door. "Hey! I'm sorry I'm late, I..." I started to say, but stopped when I saw him. His face was soaked with sweat and he looked slightly agitated. "No problem. No problem at all." He said, ushering me inside.

In the kitchen, there was only a single light on, above the table. **At it, Mrs. Lopez was writing something feverishly on a slip of paper.**

"I'll...be right back. I have to say goodbye to Denise." Denise was their one-year-old daughter, who I had been watching for them. She disappeared into the darkness of the hallway, heading up the stairs.

"What movie are you seeing tonight?" I asked, setting my bag down on the table. **The pad of paper had holes punctured through it, as if Mrs. Lopez had been pressing the pen down hard.**

"Uh? I don't know. I guess we'll decide when we get there." Mr. Lopez was shifting from foot to foot, looking more worried by the minute. I noticed a pretty sizeable cut on his

最後一次當保姆

我走到門前,看了看錶。遲到了十分鐘。我已替他們當臨時保姆六個月了,相信他們不會因而生氣。

Lopez 先生替我開門。「唏,很抱歉我遲到了,我⋯⋯」我開口說話,看見 Lopez 先生後卻說不上話了。他汗流滿面,看起來有點焦躁不安。「沒關係,真的沒關係。」他邊說邊請我進去。

廚房只有桌上的那一盞燈亮著。**我看見 Lopez 太太正忙亂地在桌面的紙條上書寫著。**

「我⋯⋯很快就回來,我要先跟 Denise 道別。」Denise 是他們一歲的女兒,也是他們需要我看管的對象。Lopez 太太漸漸消失在昏暗的走廊之中,走上了樓梯。

「你們今晚要看哪齣電影呢?」我把袋子放到桌上時問道。**紙條上穿了很多個小洞,看來 Lopez 太太寫字很用力。**

「呃,還沒想好呢,我們到了那邊再決定看哪齣吧。」Lopez 先生一直把重心從一隻腳轉移到另一隻腳,愈來愈焦急。我注意到他的右臉頰上有道頗長的傷口,而且血痕已經乾掉了。

right cheek, dribbled with dried blood.

"Are you okay, Mr. Lopez?" I asked, but before he could answer, I heard Mrs. Lopez returning from upstairs. "We...we should get going. Goodbye, Katy."

She said, pulling me into a hug. She tightened her grip for a moment and I could have sworn I heard a soft sob. *"Thank you...for everything."* She said with great difficulty.

She began to say something else but her husband grabbed her and dragged her out the door. Before he closed it, he gave me a mournful, almost apologetic look. Then he closed it, and I was alone in the dark house.

I thought about going out and talking to them more or maybe even just leaving but in the end I decided to stay.

Not turning on the lights so as to not startle up Denise, I climbed the stairs in the dark and headed into her room. I approached the crib and was about to lift her up **when I saw a note laying on top of the blankets.** I read it by the streetlight that glared feebly through the window.

「Lopez 先生，你還好嗎？」我問道，可是在他回答我之前，Lopez 太太已從樓上下來，並說：「我們……我們該走了。再見了，Katy。」

她說罷便把我拉過去擁抱，有一下子抱得特別緊，而且我發誓，我聽見她嗚咽了一下。「*謝謝你……謝謝你所做的一切。*」她艱難地說出這句話。

Lopez 太太想再開口說話，可是被 Lopez 先生抓住了，還把她拉到了門外。Lopez 先生臨關門前還展露了一個很悲痛、帶點抱歉的表情。門關上了，只剩下我獨留在這間昏暗的房子裏。

我有想過出去找他們多說一些話，甚至有想過直接離開房子，不過我最後還是決定留下來。

我不想驚醒 Denise，所以沒有開燈。我摸黑地爬上樓梯，走向她的房間。我靠近了嬰兒床，正想抱起她之際，**看見了被子上有一張字條**。只靠窗外透進來的微弱街燈，我勉強地讀著字條上的字。

Katy, I'm so sorry. He broke in while we were getting ready. He said he was going to kill us. Do horrible things to Denise. He asked if anyone knew about us and we told him about you. It's an exchange. I'm so sorry. I hope that God will forgive me one day.

Looking out the window, I saw them pulling out of the driveway. They were crying. Perched in Mrs. Lopez's lap was Denise.

Behind me, in the darkness, the door creaked open.

*Katy，我很抱歉，他在我們準備出門時闖了進來。他揚言要
把我們殺掉，還會對 Denise 做出可怕的事。他問有沒有認
識我們的人，我們跟他談起了你……這是個交易，我真的很
抱歉。願上帝寬恕我。*

我望向窗外，看見他們正在離開車道。他們都在哭。在
Lopez 太太腿上的，正是 Denise。

而我身後的漆黑，傳來了「*吱嘎*」的開門聲。

He Took Me to the Lake

I really wasn't expecting the invitation, but it was one that I couldn't refuse. After all, he was the brother of my best friend.

Him and I had never quite seen eye to eye, and I always felt as if he resented me for being his brother's best friend. Honestly, it was only at his brother's funeral that he really opened up to me, and I think we really bonded over the memories we shared of his presumed to be dead brother.

See, my best friend had gone missing several weeks ago and it was only recently that the authorities had finally decided that all of their resources had been exhausted, and called off the search.

We both took it fairly hard, and I think that made us turn to each other for comfort, so when he invited me to go fishing with him I was more than happy to go.

But my enthusiasm clouded my judgement.

I should've been suspicious when he told me the cinderblock and rope were to make a makeshift anchor for the rowboat.

他帶我到湖邊

我真的沒想到他會約我,不過他始終是我最好朋友的弟弟嘛,我也不好意思拒絕。

我跟他一直以來也不是特別投契,我總覺得他因為我是他哥哥的最好朋友,而對我抱有怨恨。

老實說,到了他哥哥的喪禮上,他跟我說出了一切,那時我才明白,那些我們分別擁有、與他亡兄有關的回憶和經歷,使我和他的關係變得密切。

我最好的朋友幾個星期前失蹤了,直到最近,當局才終於宣布由於他們已經用盡方法,但仍徒勞無功,於是終止了搜查。

我和弟弟都感到很傷痛,這令我們不自覺地,想要從對方身上得到安慰,所以當他邀請我一起去釣魚時,我立即答應了。

可是我開心過頭了,使我的判斷力減弱了很多。

當他告訴我那磚塊和繩索是要為划艇做一個臨時錨時,我早該起疑了。

I should've been quicker when he grabbed me by the feet and tied the other end of the rope to my legs.

I should've been stronger and grabbed on to the side of the boat as he threw me overboard.

They say that when you die your life flashes before your eyes, but instead I was greeted by a familiar face.

Sure, the weeks underwater had distorted his features a little, but I would recognize the face of my best friend anywhere.

I always figured I would die with my mind at peace, but in the last moments before my world turned black, my mind was aflame with a burning question.

How did he know that this is where I left his brother, when I took him to the lake, all those weeks ago.

當他抓住我的腳，並將繩子的另一端綁在我的腿上時，我的動作應該要比他更快。

當他把我扔到船外時，我應該要更有力地抓住船邊。

人們說當你快要死的時候，你的一生會像走馬燈般在你的眼前閃現，可是現在我只看到一張熟悉的面孔。

浸泡在水底幾個星期後，他的臉理所當然地有少許扭曲了，但我還是能認出這是我最好的朋友。

我本以為自己會在心無雜念的情況下死去，但在世界變黑之前的最後時刻，我的腦海裏浮現出一道縈繞不休的問題——

他怎麼會知道，幾個星期前，正是我把他哥哥帶到這裏？

Daisy

Daisy died fifteen years ago. I make a point of it to visit her grave as often as possible.

It's a long drive. I try to pass the time by thinking of happier times—meeting Daisy for the first time, our weekend at the cabin—but it fills me with regret. These trips always fill me with regret.

But I have to do this. Even if it means going 90 in a 55 mile per hour zone. Even if it means nearly smacking into a moped driver who has no business being in the left lane. The sooner I get there, the better.

Eventually I exit off the highway onto an old country road, kicking up brick-red dust along the way. Farther down the road is the lakeside cabin where we spent our single, impromptu weekend together. The owners of the cabin never stayed there or rented it out to anyone, she insisted.

"I'm sure we could find plenty of use for this old cabin," she'd said with a wink.

Regret starts to kick in more and more as I near the cabin. I never meant for things to escalate the way they did that weekend. It was one of those romances where the iron got hot too early.

雛菊

十五年前，Daisy 去世了。這些年來，我一直堅持花時間到
她的墓穴拜祭。

車程很遙遠，為了打發時間，我試著在腦海裏回想一些快樂
時光，例如與 Daisy 初次在小屋見面的那個週末，但每次回
憶起總令我感到懊悔；每次過來的這段路程總讓我感到遺憾。

但我不得不這樣做，即使我在限速五十五英里的路段把車開
到時速九十英里也好；即使那個駛在左線、無辜的摩托車司
機差點兒被我撞飛也好；我也要盡快到達。

終於駛離漫長的高速公路，進入古老的鄉村道路，揚起了路
上磚紅色的塵土。沿路再往下走，就是我和 Daisy 一起度過
那個即慶週末的湖邊小屋了。她堅稱小屋的主人從不會這裏
過夜，也不會把小屋租給別人。

「我相信我們定能把這間老舊小屋活用得淋漓盡致呢！」她
向我打眼色道。

現在我走得愈近小屋，懊悔的情緒就愈強烈。我從沒想過那
個週末的事情會發展得這般急速，本來應是打得火熱的浪漫
情節，突然變得失控。

Or, in Daisy's instance, bludgeoned the back of her head.

19 Piedmont Place. This is the cabin. Her grave is marked by a plot of fresh, healthy daisies. Good to see that the absentee owners are at least employing someone to tend the garden.

Of all my regrets, I think the biggest is that I never learned her real name. It's a problem that I have. Things always escalate too quickly for me and I become too infatuated to concern myself with certain details, even major ones like names.

Then again, there are things about myself I simply can't change. This is what I am.

On that note, I suppose it's time I pay Violet a visit.

然而，對 Daisy 來說，她沒有想過的，是後腦的一記重擊。

Piedmont Place 19 號，正是小屋所在的位置。她的墓穴上放滿了茁壯的鮮雛菊，很是顯眼。雖然小屋的主人經常不在，可是他至少也有請人來看顧花園，我很是替他高興。

在我眾多的遺憾當中，最讓我耿耿於懷的，是我無法得知她真實的名字。這是我的缺點。事情往往都發展得太快，我太著迷了，使我忽略了很多細節，就連名字這麼重要的資訊，也被我忽略了。

事到如今，有很多事實都不可能再改變了，包括我的本性。

說到這裏，我想是時候去探訪一下 Violet 了。

If You Hear a Child Crying Alone at Night, Run

"If you hear a kid out around the corner woods crying for help, ignore it, especially at night." That was what uncle Stevie told my brother and I as children, and to anyone new that walked into his local watering hole.

His go-to story was when he was 25 and allegedly followed the sound of crying to what looked like a boy huddling on the ground in jeans and a red t-shirt, cradling what appeared to be a broken wrist and arm. When uncle Stevie stooped down to him, he noticed that the boy's clothes were just colored fine hairs surrounding a mouth that started at his shoulders and ended at the "feet". Stevie ran off from this "bait", and told the story ever since to anyone and everyone. His story spread like wildfire.

I never believed in a thing that mimics a hurt boy to eat people, and I thought the entire thing was made up by my uncle to get a little fame around town. My brother, however, believed Stevie's story like holy doctrine.

To settle it, we went out to the woods many times to find this boy, despite our uncle warning us not to. We always found nothing, and argued that the sound of us arguing was chasing it away, so we parted ways to explore our own section of the woods, and agreed to return home by 5.

別理會叢林裏的求救聲

「如果你聽到有孩子在叢林一角喊救命，特別是在晚上聽見的話，千萬別管他。」 Stevie 叔叔當時這樣警剔著還是小孩的我和弟弟，還跟他酒吧裏每一位新客人都說過。

叔叔之所以言之鑿鑿，源於他自稱曾追尋過這個哭喊聲的故事。那時他二十五歲。走到叢林裏的他，看到一個穿著紅色上衣和牛仔褲的男孩蜷縮在地上，輕輕抱著不知道是斷掌還是斷臂的東西。叔叔蹲下來仔細一看，才發現男孩的衣服，原來只是一團纏在嘴邊，染了紅色的細毛，由胳膊一直延伸至那似腿非腿的部分。叔叔落荒而逃，丟下這塊「誘餌」。之後他將這次經歷告知每一個人，故事如野火般迅速傳開。

我不相信有任何東西會為了吃人而佯裝成受傷的男孩，我倒覺得只是叔叔胡謅來讓自己在鎮上得到一點名氣而已，但弟弟卻把故事當作教條一樣深信不疑。

不管叔叔的多番警告，我們為了追尋真相，曾經多次走入叢林，試圖找出那個「男孩」。多次搜尋不果後，我們開始指摘是對方的談話聲把男孩給嚇走。我們最後只好決定分開行動，各自搜索一邊叢林，並於五點回家碰面。

By 5, my brother had not returned home. I had to lie when questioned- nobody could know we were even CLOSE to the corner woods, and I feared punishment more than I feared my pigheaded brother's well-being. I also figured that the "woods" we were in was a patch of man-made "forest" less than an acre big between a few large apartment buildings and a supermarket. Even IF my brother was hurt, I figured someone would come along and find him.

But my brother did not return. When the police questioned me, I said I didn't know anything. They didn't press a 7 year old.

They found my brother the next morning. He had fallen in gap in the earth and wedged himself in, leaving only his head and a bit of hand exposed. He broke his arm in the process, leaving him defenseless against the crows that had picked most of his skull clean.

I learned later that at least 20 people had heard a boy crying for help that night. One even remembered my brother saying that his arm was broken. All of them said they avoided the cries because of my uncle Stevie's story.

五點了，弟弟還沒有回來。有人問起時我只好撒謊，絕對不能讓任何人知道我們曾經接近叢林，甚至深入其中探險！比起蠢蛋弟弟的安危，我更擔心會被罰。而且我發現那所謂的「叢林」只不過是片不足一英畝大、位於幾棟住宅和超市中間的人造森林而已。即使、萬一他受傷了，我想總有人會經過而且找得到他。

但他沒有回來。當警察前來盤問我的時候，我說自己一無所知。他們不會向一個七歲的孩子逼供。

就在翌日，他們找到了弟弟。弟弟剛好掉進了在一個土地的空隙裏，只剩下頭和一小部分的手露在外面。他在跌下來的時候摔斷了手臂，完全無法抵住烏鴉的攻勢，最後被叼咬得一乾二淨，幾乎只剩下一副顱骨。

後來我才知道，**當晚至少有二十個人聽見男孩的呼救聲，其中一個甚至記得弟弟在喊自己摔斷了手。可是他們每一個都迴避了，只因為聽過 Stevie 叔叔說的故事。**

Stranger Danger

It seems like everyone's talking about Stranger Danger these days. But the best advice I've ever heard? Tell your kids that if they're ever lost in a public place, like the mall, and they can't find a police officer, **they should look for a mom with kids, and ask her for help.**

I love that idea. Finally, some positive, concrete advice, instead of all the negatives: don't talk to strangers, don't let anyone touch you, don't, don't, don't!

Sometimes kiddos just need to hear that there really are people out there that they can trust. Not everyone's a monster. As a single woman with young children, we all need a little help sometimes, right?

I mean, come on, with this crazy bunch, just the thought of a mall makes me tired!

I have enough trouble getting the kids out of their room, and then I have to put them into some decent clothes and brush their hair. God forbid I forget to feed them before we leave, or it'll be endless begging for giant pretzels and fro-yo. And once we're finally at the mall (hallelujah!), I have to constantly threaten them, just to get them to act normal.

生人勿近

最近似乎每個人都在說「生人勿近」，但是你知道我聽過最好的建議是甚麼嗎？如果你的孩子在公共場所（例如商場）走失的話，教導他們要是找不到警察，就應該去找那些帶著孩子的媽媽，並向她們尋求幫助。

我覺得這真是個好主意！討論了那麼久，終於有一些積極和具體的建議，而不是一面倒的負面駁斥：不要與陌生人交談，不要讓任何人觸摸你，全都是不要，不要，不要！

有時候孩子們只需要知道，這世上真的有人可以信任，不是每個人都是怪物。作為帶著小孩的單身女性，我們有時也需要一些幫助啊，對吧？

我是說，得了吧，雖然說了一堆亂七八糟的胡話，可是我光是想到要去商場就覺得累了！

要孩子們離開房間已經讓我費盡心神了，接著還要幫他們穿上體面的衣服、幫他們梳頭髮。出門之前，千萬不能忘了要先餵飽孩子們，否則他們會無止境地乞求想要吃巨型椒鹽脆餅乾和乳酪雪糕。當我們終於到達商場的時候（萬歲！），為了讓他們乖乖的，我得經常威脅他們。

But oh lord, all my frustrations evaporate when I'm finally walking hand-in-hand with the children, past all those stores full of families whose kids are running wild, just itching to wander off and get lost. That's when all my effort transforms into beautiful, golden possibility.

It makes everything worth it if I can bring home another one.

可是，天啊，當我終於和孩子們一起挽著手逛街時，尤其是經過那些充斥著一家大小的商店，看著那些孩子東奔西跑時，快要跟家人走散了然後迷路的天真模樣，我所有的挫敗感統統都消失了。我付出的所有努力，正是用來換取這些美好的黃金機會啊。

如果我可以多把一個小孩帶回家的話，那一切都值得了。

Stay Alert
別 掉 以 輕 心

Your Face Gives It Away

I'm having dinner in a dark quiet restaurant. My waiter comes over to ask if I'd like dessert. I look up at his face. I haven't met him before this night, but I already know that he cheated on his wife while she was dying of cancer. I look down at my empty plate and tell him no thanks.

After leaving the restaurant, I head down the street, keeping my gaze away from other people. I try not to look, but it's impossible most of the time. Too tempting. I glance at the faces of the others who are passing me on the sidewalk, and **suddenly I know their secrets.**

"Skipped his dad's funeral to get drunk at a bar"
"Stealing money from her clients"
"Lost his virginity to a prostitute"

They're all written clearly on everyone's faces. The deepest darkest secrets they have, in full display on their foreheads. No one else can see them of course. I don't know why I have this ability, but I would give anything to get rid of it. Imagine knowing the worst thing you could possibly know about someone within seconds of meeting them. Admittedly, there are some boring secrets (I wanted to hug the old woman whose worst secret was that she had sex once before getting married yet still wore white to her wedding) but there are some truly fucking horrible secrets.

相由心生

我正在一家既黑暗又安靜的餐廳吃飯。服務員過來問我需不需要吃甜點。我抬頭看著他的臉。我在今晚之前沒有見過他，但我已經知道他在患癌的妻子瀕死時出了軌。我低頭看著我的空盤子，跟他說「不用了，謝謝」。

離開餐廳後，我沿著街道走，同時努力不注視其他人。我盡量都不去看別人，但大部分時間還是忍不住看了，因為他們太誘人了。我匆匆看過那些在人行道上，跟我擦肩而過的路人的臉，**我瞬間便知道了他們的秘密**。

「因為在酒吧買醉而缺席了父親的葬禮」
「偷了客人的錢」
「把童貞獻給了妓女」

這些秘密都清楚地寫在每個人的臉上。人們最黑暗、最不可告人的秘密，我都能在他們的額頭上一覽無遺，當然只有我才能看得見。我不知道自己為甚麼會有這種能力，但我卻不顧一切也想擺脫它。試想像一下，你遇到人們的幾秒鐘內，你便可能知道他們最糟糕的事情了。有些人的確藏著一些無聊的秘密（我遇過一位老婦人，她最大的秘密是她在結婚之前，曾經有過一次性行為，可是她在自己的婚禮上還是穿了象徵純潔的白色婚紗，我真想給她一個擁抱），但是有些人的秘密是真正他媽的可怕。

Forget about dating. I tried a few times, but seeing a woman's baggage immediately on the first date killed the attraction for me. There was Naomi, whose face told me that she secretly believed that white people are superior to all other races. Then there was Eve, who apparently was a lesbian repressing her sexuality to appease her strict parents. My last date was with a woman named Jamie, who had a fetish that was so disturbing and illegal that it still haunts me to this day. It's a hard fucking way to live, to say the least.

As I walk down the street, I'm getting overwhelmed by all the people around me, their faces advertising their sinister secrets as they walk ignorantly along. This anxiety I'm feeling happens a lot. I barely go out anymore. I've been planning to break my lease so I can move to a secluded area, where I can live my life while having minimal contact with other people. I walk to a quiet side street and request an Uber on my phone. He arrives a minute later and I dive in, relieved to be going home.

"How's your night going?" the driver asks me, turning around in his seat.

My throat tightens up as I see *"killed his last two passengers"* scrawled on his forehead. He turns back around and slams on the gas.

看到路人已經這麼壓抑了，更別說要約會了。我約會過好幾個女生，可是第一次見面就立刻看到對方的思想包袱，甚麼吸引力也沒了。Naomi 的臉告訴我，她暗地裏相信白人比其他所有種族也優越。接下來有 Eve，她顯然是一個女同性戀者，可是為了滿足她那對嚴格父母的期望，只好隱瞞自己的性取向。我最後約會過的女生叫 Jamie，她的癖好令人非常不安，而且是非法的，至今仍困擾著我。我真的沒有誇張，我的生活好像調到「困難模式」般難熬。

當我走在街上時，我被周圍的所有人淹沒了，他們只是在走路，可是他們的臉卻不斷展示著險惡的秘密。這讓我感到焦慮，所以我現在幾乎都不會出門了。我有打算違反租約條例，希望可以藉此搬到一個僻靜的地方，然後我就可以在那裏過上孤寡的生活，再也不用與其他人頻繁接觸。我走到一條安靜的小街上，用手機叫了車子。一分鐘後車子就到了，我鑽進車廂，想著可以回家實在是太好，也讓我鬆了一口氣。

「你的晚上過得好嗎？」司機轉頭向我問道。

當我看到他額頭上潦草地寫著「*殺死了上兩名乘客*」時，我快要窒息了。他轉回頭，猛地踩下油門。

Give Me a Smile

"Come on, give me a smile." smirked the Jerk that has come by my work for the 8th time.
"You'd look prettier." he adds.

I sigh and continue on with my wheelbarrow.

That's one of the downsides of here, any creep that wants to can stroll straight into my life. Don't get me wrong, I love working at the zoo. I get to take care of spectacular animals, feeding the big cats is my favourite.

I get harassed a lot, and it doesn't faze me much anymore. However, there is something about this one that feels different. I actually knew of this particular Jerk, friend of a friend of a friend kind of thing. So, I knew a few things about him. None of them good.

'It is a little annoying how good looking he is for a creep.' involuntarily passes through my brain.

The 9th time he came by was when it happened.

笑一個吧

「來嘛，笑一個吧。」在我工作時走來搭話的蠢蛋假笑著說，今次已是第八次。

「你笑起來更好看啊。」他補充道。

我嘆了口氣，然後繼續推著手推車。

那些想入侵我生活的討厭鬼，都可以直接跟我接觸，這可算是在這裏工作的壞處之一。別誤會我的意思，我很喜歡在動物園工作。我可以照顧這些讓人嘆為觀止的動物，餵飼那些大型貓科動物更是我最愛的工序呢。

我經常受到騷擾，所以我現在已經不會覺得驚慌失措了。然而，他讓我覺得這次有點不一樣。我其實是認識這個蠢蛋的，他算是我朋友的朋友的朋友吧。所以我只知道很少關於他的事情，但當中沒有一樣是正面的。

「討厭鬼來說，他長得有點太帥了吧，真是惱人呢⋯⋯」這個想法不由自主地在我腦海中浮現。

他第九次來的時候，就發生了以下的事情。

Towards the end of a very long day was when he cornered me. Impeding my travel with his arm outstretched against the wall. Indecently close to me, I could smell his aftershave and feel his breath.

"Hey pretty lady, you're such a tease." I hear.

There was still so much to do before going home and my mind was oddly fuzzy. Like I was passenger and not driver in my body.

"Sorry, I'm errr, quite busy." I gulp as my vision goes hazy for a second.Before I know it, he leans in and kisses me, catching me completely off guard.

'Fuck it' I think, 'it has been a while, why not?' as I regain my composure and kiss him back.

We quickly move through the door behind me. The "staff only" sign, completely ignored.

After a few minutes I break away, a huge toothy grin on my face.

"I told you you'd look prettier if you sm..."

漫長的一天快要結束時，他攔住了我。他伸出手臂把我逼在牆角，不讓我繼續走。然後毫不客氣地靠近我，近得我聞到他臉上鬍後水的味道，也感受到他的鼻息。

「嘿，美女，你好風騷喔！」我聽見他這樣說。

在下班回家之前，還有很多事情等著我去完成，但我的思緒怪異地模糊了起來。就像是靈魂出竅了般，身體變得不由自主。

「抱歉，我……呃……挺忙的。」剛剛視力朦朧了一下，我緊張得倒吸了一口氣。我反應過來之前，他已經靠近我並吻了下來，讓我完全措手不及。

「管他的……」我心想，「都已經一段時間了，何不試試看？」我冷靜下來並迎上了他的吻。

我們快速穿過身後的門，完全無視了寫著「非工作人員禁止進出」的標誌。

幾分鐘後，我掙脫了，臉上掛著大大的露齒笑容。

「我就說嘛，你笑起來更好……」

Brzzzz Brzzzz my alarm interrupts his now slightly amusing comment.

"Ohh fuck, its 10pm. I need to lock up right away." I say slightly panicked "I'll be right back." I add with a quick peck.

Leaving quickly through the heavy steel reinforced door, he doesn't notice as I turn the key and press a few buttons.

I know this aggressive Jerk is intending to cheat on his girlfriend. I know lots of things he doesn't think are important, like how in the animal kingdom a smile has a very different meaning.

A smile is a show of teeth, a warning.

I take my place on the other side of the glass enclosure, with some popcorn and a slush puppy. I always did like feeding the big cats.

1 cheater and 4 cheetahs in a cage. one of them screaming to be let out, four of them with big hungry tooth filled smiles.

I can't help myself as I shout "Come on, give me a smile!"

「嘶嘶——」我的鬧鐘打斷了他現在這個挺有趣的描述。

「噢靠!晚上十點了。我要立刻去上鎖。」我有點恐慌地說道:「我很快回來。」我輕吻了他的一下才離開。

他沒有注意到我轉動鑰匙並按下幾個按鈕的動作,我飛快地穿過了沉重的加固鋼門。

我知道這個進取的蠢蛋打算背叛女朋友,我也知道很多他認為不重要的事情,譬如說,在動物界中,微笑的含義是截然不同的。

微笑,是露出牙齒,是一種警告。

我在玻璃幕牆的另一邊找了個位置坐下來,還準備好了爆米花和汽水。我總是很喜歡餵飼那些大型貓科動物。

一個「獵炮」的人和四隻獵豹同在一個籠子裏,其中一個尖叫著想要出來,其餘四隻正飢腸轆轆、齜牙咧嘴地笑著。

我按捺不住地大喊道:「來嘛,笑一個啊!」

Father

"Goodbye Sister Claire! I shall see you tomorrow!" Father Markus called out whilst locking the church doors. He had been there since 6am and with his old age the long days have been taking a toll on him. He was glad the day was nearly at and end and he could rest.

"Father…" a voice whimpered out.
"Ohh, you startled me child. Come closer, this old man doesn't see well."

A man stepped from the shadows. He was tall and unkempt and fidgeting at his jacket.

"Is there something I can help you with? I'm afraid I've just locked up, so you'd have to come back tomorrow if it is confession you seek."

"No father, not confession." The man pulled a cigarette from his jacket and Father Markus noticed his hands. The tall man was shaking uncontrollably, finding it impossible to light his cigarette.

"My poor man, you are terrified. What is it? Tell me what haunts you. "
"There's something inside me. Making me do… unspeakable things. I can't control it. I don't want to do the things it tells

神父

「再見了，Claire 修女！我們明天再會！」Markus 神父把教堂門鎖上時喊道。他從早上六點開始就一直待在那邊，隨著年齡的增長，早出晚歸的生活漸漸對他造成負面的影響。他很高興這一天快要結束了，他終於可以休息了。

「神父……」有把聲音嗚咽著說。
「噢，你讓我吃了一驚呢，孩子。走近一點，我這位老人看東西不太清楚。」

一個男人從陰暗處走了出來。蓬頭垢面的他身材高大，玩弄著自己的夾克。

「我有甚麼可以幫你的嗎？可是我已經把門鎖起來了，所以如果你是想來懺悔的話，你要明天才過來呢。」

「不是的，神父，不是懺悔。」男子從夾克裏拿了一根煙出來，Markus 神父注意到了他的手。那個高個子男人的手無法控制地顫抖著，抖得點不到香煙。

「可憐的孩子，你很害怕呢。發生甚麼事了？把你的困擾告訴我吧。」
「我內心有些東西。要我做出一些……不能言喻的事情。我無法控制它，我不想做它要我做的事情。」

me."

"It speaks to you son?" Markus had heard of many cases of possession but never before seen one first hand.

"Yes. All the time, and it shows me horrible visions… such terrible things."

"Listen to me child. I will help you with this demon. You are not alone on this journey."

"No, no… **it is not a demon. It is god.**"

"No child, God would not make you enact these terrible acts and fill your head with nightmarish visions. This sounds like a demon. Demons are master deceivers."

"He shows me the truth, the evil in humanity… such terrible things. He is not deceitful, only vengeful, and he has showed who you really are."

"Child, you do not know what you're saying." Father Markus felt scared now.

"How you could you do that? They were so young, so innocent."

Father Markus was stunned and took a step back. "No, I… I… It can't be."

「它跟你説話了嗎，孩子？」Markus 聽説過許多被惡魔纏身的案例，但從未親身接觸過。

「是的。每分每秒也在跟我説話，它向我展示了很多可怕的景象……那些糟糕的事情。」

「聽我説吧，孩子。我會幫助你驅走這個惡魔。在這趟旅程中，你並不孤單。」

「不，不……**那不是惡魔，那是上帝。**」

「不是的，孩子。上帝不會強迫你看見這些可怕的行為，也不會使你的腦袋充滿噩夢般的異象。你這個情況聽起來像是被惡魔纏身吧。惡魔很擅長迷惑人類的呢。」

「祂向我展示了真相，人類邪惡的一面……那些糟糕的事情。祂不是想迷惑我，只是一心想報復，祂還向我展示了你的真面目。」

「孩子，你在亂説甚麼啊？」Markus 神父現在感到害怕了。**「你怎麼做得出這種事？他們都很年輕，很無辜。」**

Markus 神父驚呆了，後退了一步，「不，我……我……不可能。」

The man pulled a knife from his jacket, and a tear ran down his cheek.

"You see why I have to kill you, don't you?"

"No, no, please God, please forgive me for what I have done." Markus knelt down and began to weep.

The man stared down at him. "He doesn't."

那個男人從夾克裏掏出一把刀，淚水順著他的臉頰流下來。

「你明白為甚麼我要殺了你吧，對嗎？」

「不，不，上帝，請原諒我所做的事。」Markus 跪在地上，並哭泣起來。

那個男人低頭看著他：「他不會。」

There, there...

The sound of whistling snapped Chloe out of her micro-sleep, and reality flooded back. The tears, the screaming, and above all else the feeling of complete exhaustion. She hadn't had a good night's sleep since Jess was born.

"There, there…" Chloe calmly whispered as she rocked Jess in her arms. "Are you hungry?"

Jess's screams were confirmation enough. Chloe filled Jess's formula bottle and began the arduous feeding process. Like always, as soon as the bottle hit Jess's lips she struggled and wriggled in Chloe's arms, **but this time worse than ever.**

"There, there..." Chloe drifted back to a mindless daze and Jess soon stopped struggling.

A slow burning pain jolted Chloe out of her micro-sleep, and reality flooded back. The tears, the screaming, and above all else the feeling of complete shock.

She hadn't let the water cool.

喝吧喝吧

汽笛聲把 Chloe 從微睡中喚醒過來,催促她回到現實。那些眼淚、那些尖叫聲,以上種種加起來,就等於徹底筋疲力盡。自 Jess 出生以來,她沒有一晚睡得安穩。

「好啦,好啦⋯⋯」Chloe 冷靜地低聲說道,她輕輕搖晃著懷內的 Jess。「你餓了嗎?」

Jess 的哭喊聲足以確認了 Chloe 的設想。Chloe 把 Jess 的奶瓶裝滿了,接著便開始艱辛的餵食過程。一如以往,當瓶子一碰到 Jess 的嘴唇,她就會在 Chloe 的懷抱中不斷掙扎扭動,**可是這次 Jess 比之前更用力掙扎。**

「好啦,好啦⋯⋯」神情恍惚的 Chloe,意識再次飄走了,Jess 亦很快安靜了下來。

一陣緩慢的灼熱痛感讓 Chloe 從微睡中醒來過來,催促她回到現實。那些眼淚、那些尖叫聲,以上種種加起來,就等於徹底的震驚。

她忘了把水放涼。

Naomi Losing Teeth

My daughter, Naomi, lost her first tooth when she was seven. An old scholar on tales regarding the Tooth Fairy, I watched her excitedly place it beneath her pillow.

Later that night, I swapped it for a dollar underneath her soundly sleeping head. Mission accomplished – mom milestone unlocked.

Naomi chattered endlessly the next morning about how she was sure she'd seen the tooth fairy that night. I smiled inwardly, remembering her undisturbed peace.

She didn't describe what she thought she'd seen, but I imagined her head was full of pointy-eared, pastel-colored fairies, bedecked in various kinds of tooth jewelry.

Naomi continued to lose teeth, and I continued to swap them out for a dollar or some coins. Sometimes I'd throw in some international money – pesos, euros, a Canadian dollar – just to spice things up. I would shrug and tell Naomi the Tooth Fairy "must have gotten mixed up", adding to the illusion of a globetrotting pixie.

I loved how her eyes shone with the magic and mystery of it.

牙仙子傳說

女兒 Naomi 七歲時掉了第一顆牙齒。她非常熱衷於民間傳說「牙仙子」的故事，我看著她興奮地把掉了的牙齒放在枕頭下。

那天晚上，她正睡得香甜，我悄悄地把牙齒換成了一美元。任務完成──成功解鎖「媽媽里程碑」。

第二天早上，Naomi 沒完沒了地談論著自己當晚確實看到了牙仙子。她明明就睡得很安穩，沒有醒過來啊，想到這裏我不禁在心底裏發笑。

她沒有描述她以為自己看到的東西是怎麼樣的，但我想像到她的腦海裏應該滿是尖耳、色彩柔和的仙女們，穿戴著各式各樣的牙齒飾品。

隨著 Naomi 踏入換牙期，她一直掉牙齒，我就繼續把它們換成一美元或是幾個硬幣。有時候為了讓事情更有趣，我更會把錢換成其他貨幣，例如比索、歐元、加元等等。要是 Naomi 問到的話，我就會聳聳肩告訴她「牙仙子一定是混淆了」，來增添「它」是一隻遊遍世界的小仙子的錯覺。

我很喜歡看到她因牙仙子的魔力和神秘感著迷時，那雙眼睛閃耀著期盼的模樣。

I remember how I felt when I first saw foreign currencies, holding the oddly-sized coins and thinking of how many miles they had traveled to get to me. I thought Naomi liked it too, **because she continued to claim she saw the tooth fairy somewhat regularly.**

When Naomi was twelve, she woke us one night screaming at the top of her lungs. When we burst into her room, we saw her sitting hunched on her bed in the corner, arms wrapped protectively around her legs.

When she lifted her face, wailing, there was blood dripping out of her mouth and down her chin. She looked like one of those B-horror child zombies – the ones who turn at the very beginning, before the parents, as to ensure an appropriate rush of sympathy from the audience.

We ran to her, and I noticed that it was cold and the window was open. I cradled my baby, touched her arms and legs and precious head to check for injuries.

There were none that I could find, just the blood from her mouth.

I stroked her head. I tried to somehow blend calmness and urgency when I said, "Sweetheart, what happened? Tell us."

我記得小時候第一次收到牙仙子送我的外幣時，我拿著那些大大小小的硬幣，想著仙子們走了多遠才能來到我身邊。所以我想 Naomi 應該也會喜歡這個情景吧，**因為她還是對我們說，她經常看到牙仙子。**

Naomi 十二歲的時候，有一晚她失聲尖叫著，驚醒了我和丈夫。我們衝進她的房間，看到她瑟縮在床的角落，雙臂環抱著腿。

她抬起頭，淚流滿面，嘴巴滴著血，流到了下巴。她看起來像是那些低成本喪屍影片裏出現的角色——那些在影片一開始就在父母面前轉過頭來現身的喪屍小孩，來適當地博取觀眾的同情。

我們跑到她身邊，我注意到房間很冷，而且窗戶打開了。我輕輕抱著我心愛的女兒，撫摸著她的手腳跟寶貴的頭部，檢查著她有沒有受傷。

除了她口中的鮮血，沒有其他異樣。

我輕撫著她的頭，試圖冷靜地表達事情的迫切性：「親愛的，發生甚麼事了？跟爸爸媽媽說吧。」

Through her gasping sobs, Naomi said that she had seen the tooth fairy outside her window tonight, and she'd told them that she was sorry but she hadn't lost a tooth recently. Then, her little brow furrowed, and she looked at her hands.

"Then what, sweetheart? It's okay, you can tell us," my husband said gently.

Naomi looked up, her face twisted in pain. In a tone that indicated she felt the answer was obvious, she whispered, "So he broke the window and took one anyway."

Naomi 氣喘吁吁地嗚咽著，說她剛剛在窗外看到了牙仙子，她對仙子們說她很抱歉，可是她最近真的沒有掉牙齒了。說完以後，她皺起眉頭，低頭看著自己的手。

「然後怎樣了呢，親愛的？放心告訴爸爸媽媽啊。」丈夫溫柔地説。

Naomi 再次抬起頭，五官因痛楚而扭成一團。她覺得答案已經很明顯了，於是她冷冷地低聲道：「然後它就打破了窗戶，強行拿走了一顆啊。」

Twenty Years in the Dark

My brother Pete disappeared twenty years ago on Halloween night. I thought I knew right where he was--hiding in our bedroom, waiting to scare me in his little Dracula costume. But when I kicked open the door to scare him first, he was gone. The only clue was a sheet of his math homework, **torn out of his notebook and left on my bed,** propped up on the pillow.

The police believed Pete had been kidnapped, and that he'd left his homework as a clue to his abductor's identity. Naturally, they zeroed in on his math teacher. There wasn't any real proof, but everyone was convinced he was guilty. The poor guy eventually left town, taking all his supposed knowledge of the whereabouts of Pete's body with him.

But I knew my brother. The kid was constantly forgetting things, tripping over nothing, getting locked out of the house. **He just wasn't quick-witted enough to leave a clue like that.**

Maybe it bugged me that everyone blamed the math teacher, or maybe I just got hooked on the excitement--whatever it was, I grew up and became a cop.

This Halloween, we got some reports about trespassers at the old Boys' Home, an abandoned building in the woods

被困黑暗二十年

我的弟弟 Pete 在二十年前的萬聖夜失蹤了。我以為我會知道他在哪裏——躲在我們的睡房裏，穿著他的小吸血鬼服裝等著嚇唬我。可是當我踢開門想先嚇唬他時，他不見了。唯一的線索是他的數學功課，**那是從他的筆記本上撕下來的一頁紙**，放了在我床上的枕頭旁邊。

警察認為 Pete 被綁架了，而他留下了的功課，就是用來表示綁架者的身份。順理成章地，警察把注意力都集中於他的數學老師身上。雖然沒有任何實質的證據，但每個人都深信他就是綁匪。這個可憐的傢伙最終被迫離開了小鎮，連同他知道 Pete 下落的所有資訊都一併帶走了。

但我很了解我的弟弟。這個孩子經常忘東忘西，又笨拙得會自己絆倒自己，或是被鎖在房子外面。**他不會機靈得留下這樣的線索。**

也許每個人都在責怪數學老師這件事讓我很困擾，或者我只是迷上了追查真相的刺激感……不管是甚麼原因也好，我長大後當上了警察。

今年萬聖節，我們收到了有人擅闖舊男童院的舉報，那是在學校後方樹林，一棟荒廢了的建築。我前往那裏，以確保當地的孩子沒有惹到不必要的麻煩。

behind the school. I headed over there to make sure local kids weren't getting into anything they shouldn't be.

I'd walked the perimeter a few times, and was about to leave when I noticed a hole in the fence, overgrown with weeds, and hidden behind a huge oak tree. I climbed through and found an entrance to the building that opened into a long hallway with a row of doors on the left and windows on the right. The first door hung from its hinges. The second door was locked. I kicked it open. It was a closet.

Inside, curled up in the corner, was a small skeleton in a vampire costume. I knew immediately what had happened. Pete had been waiting there to scare me. He just hadn't expected the door to lock. Next to him was a notebook, with a page torn out. On the page after that, there was a note:

Meet me at the Boys' Home for a SURPRISE! Hole in the fence behind the biggest tree, go in, and it's the 2nd door on the left!

I'd been wrong about my brother. He had been clever enough to leave a clue. **He'd just ripped out the wrong page.**

我在外圍走了幾圈，正準備離開之時，我注意到籬笆上有一個長滿雜草的洞，而且是藏在一棵巨大的橡樹後面。我爬了過去，發現那裏有一個通往大樓的入口，進去後是一條長走廊，左邊有一排門，右邊是窗戶。第一扇門只靠鉸鏈懸著，快掉下來了。第二扇門是鎖了起來的，我踢開了它，原來是一個壁櫥。

壁櫥裏面，有一具穿著吸血鬼服裝的小骷髏，蜷縮在角落。我馬上就意識到發生了甚麼事。Pete 一直在那裏等著嚇唬我……他只是沒想到壁櫥門會鎖起來。在他旁邊有一本筆記本，裏面有一頁被撕走了。在那之後的一頁上，寫了些字句：

來男童院找我吧，保證有驚喜喔！最大那棵樹後面的柵欄上有個洞，走進去後，打開左邊的第二道門！

我一直都誤會了弟弟。他很聰明地留下了線索。**他只是撕了筆記本裏錯的一頁。**

The End of the Hallway

I have a long, dark hallway in my house. Before I go to bed, I always turn off the bathroom light, then the hall light, and then I walk those last few steps to my bedroom in darkness. **Some nights, I feel like something is creeping up behind me from down the hall.**

It's ridiculous, I know. I'm a grownup. So, with sensible maturity, I've always ignored the feeling. I never check over my shoulder. I just hold my breath, slip into the bedroom, and calmly shut the door.

Tonight I sensed something in the hallway again. Except it didn't creep. It ran. I heard the pounding footsteps, the air rushing past its body. I managed to get into my bedroom and close the door, just before that thing slammed into it from the other side.

I've locked the door, and pushed my dresser in front of it. The window has security bars, so going out that way isn't an option. I can't call 911, because my phone's still in the bathroom, charging. So far nobody's heard me when I scream out the window.

I'm too scared to sleep, too tired not to. I have to stay awake. I keep shouting "Go away!", and every single time, that thing smashes into my bedroom door again.

長廊的盡頭

我家中有條又長又黑暗的走廊。在我上床睡覺之前，通常都會先關掉浴室燈，然後關走廊燈，最後要摸黑走幾步到睡房。**有些晚上，我會覺得有些甚麼正從走廊裏向我身後爬過來。**

我知道這聽起來很荒謬，畢竟我已是個成年人了啊。因此，以我該有的成熟和理智，我每次都會故意忽略那個怪異的感覺。我從來不會回頭查看，我只會屏住呼吸，溜進睡房，然後靜靜地關上門。

今晚我又感覺到走廊裏有些甚麼東西，可是它沒有爬過來，而是跑起來了。我聽見它砰砰直跳的腳步聲，還感覺到在它身旁竄動的空氣。我設法走進了睡房，剛好在它來到前關上了門，使它猛地撞上了門。

我鎖上了門，接著把梳妝台推到了門前擋住。睡房的窗戶裝了安全欄，所以不能從那邊逃出去。我亦無法打電話報警，因為我的手機還在浴室裏充著電。我向窗外大喊大叫，可是到目前為止還沒有人聽見我求救。

我害怕得睡不著覺，卻同時累得很想睡。我必須保持清醒。我不斷喊著「走開！」，然而隨著我每一次叫喊，那東西都會大力撞向我的睡房門。

My voice is scratchy now from yelling.

"Go away!"

Crash.

I don't really want it to go away. I want it to keep bashing my door all night. Because, until I think of a better plan, it's better than hearing it run away down the hall, toward my baby's room.

喊了這麼久，我的嗓子現在都變得沙啞了。

「走開！」

撞擊聲。

我不是真的想它走開，我反而想它整夜都會在撞我的門。因為，在我想到更好的計劃之前，聽見它撞門，總好比聽見它沿著走廊跑向嬰兒室吧。

The Sheriff's Announcement

"Ladies and gentlemen..."

The Sheriff reluctantly began his announcement from the podium. Something untangible was stuck in his windpipes, blocking what he had to say. He cleared his throat in an awkward attempt to regain his composure.

"I am extremely sorry, once again, to have to gather everyone here to announce our findings on the latest case of thirteen missing children in our town. As a father of two, I can only imagine the pain this has brought to your families, and please accept my condolences for your lost."

He stopped. His words were engulfed by the tension and silence in the room. A single whimper flared up, and died out almost instantly.

He knew. Their pain had been pushed over the limit of endurance.

"So, let us go straight to our findings. We would like to announce that the culprit has been captured. Thanks to the locals' cooperations, we have traced the evidences to his hiding place, and..."

He stopped again. Even this, seemingly positive, news

警長的聲明

「各位先生女士們⋯⋯」

警長不情願地在講台上發表著聲明。好像有甚麼無形的東西卡在他的氣管裏，讓他很難開口宣布接下來要說的話。他尷尬地清了清嗓子，嘗試讓自己回復平靜。

「我得再次表示非常抱歉，為了發表有關鎮上十三名失蹤兒童案的調查結果，我不得不把大家聚集到這邊來。作為兩個孩子的父親，我能想像到此事為不少家庭帶來了無盡的痛苦，我為此致以深切的哀悼。」

警長停了下來。他的話被場內一片沉默的緊張氣氛所吞沒。台下傳來了一聲嗚咽，但幾乎馬上就安靜了下來。

他很清楚，家屬們的痛苦已經超過了忍耐的極限。

「那麼，我們直接宣布調查結果吧。我們已經成功逮捕肇事兇手。有賴當地居民的合作，我們才能蒐集足夠證據，並追溯到他的藏身之處⋯⋯」

他又停了下來。即使宣布了這個聽起來相當正面的消息，也無法打破場內被悲傷籠罩的氛圍。

couldn't do much to penetrate the viscous atmosphere of the room.

A few eyebrows raised, a few heads dropped; and in that posture of giving up, they quietly lowered their gaze again. They knew the next part.

"...regrettably, we have found thirteen headless bodies in his basement."

Despite having anticipated the news, people in the room could not stop themselves from shivering at the horror of it. The words busted the floodgate wide open, and the uncontrollable sobbing simultaneously started.

On top of that tragic ambience, the Sheriff cleared his throat again, trying to muster the last of his courage to finish the announcement.

"We have also found, ladies and gentlemen, and there is no other way for me to put this to you, thirteen children's heads in his chest freezer..."

He barely got his last word out before the room was flooded with screams, shouts, and more sobs. The sound rose up like a tsunami of anger and desperation. The men tried to hold

台下有些人揚起了眉，有些人則皺起了眉。心知不妙的他們開始感到絕望，又悄悄地垂下了頭。因為他們知道接下來聽到的一定是壞消息。

「……遺憾的是，我們在他的地下室裏找到了十三具無頭屍體。」

儘管場內的人們已有心理準備接受這個殘酷的消息，但聽見警長此話一出，他們還是害怕得顫抖起來。這句話像炮彈般打破家屬們強忍著淚水的眼眶，使他們開始無法自控地的抽泣著。

在這個悲慘的氣氛底下，警長再次清了清喉嚨，鼓起最後的勇氣完成是次發表。

「各位先生女士們，恕我無法用其他更婉轉含蓄的方式表達。我們另外也發現了，在兇手家中的大冰櫃中，放有十三個孩子的頭顱……」

在他吐出最後一個字之前，場內已經充斥著尖叫聲、吶喊聲和更多的飲泣聲。悲痛的哭聲集結起來，就像憤怒和絕望的海嘯般，淹沒著眾人。男人們都忙著扶持他們的妻子，又互相擁抱著，試圖從對方身上找回最後一絲理智和安慰。

on to their wives, and they embraced each other, trying to find some last drops of sanity and consolation.

"But..."

One word, one single simple syllable was all it took to reign back all the emotions and get everyone's attention. They stared in bewilderment at the podium, where the Sheriff was strained and warped under the immense invisible weight of the news.

"But, ladies and gentlemen. The thirteen heads did not match the thirteen bodies."

「可是……」

一個詞語,兩個簡單的音節,就足以重新支配在場所有人的
情緒,也奪回他們的注意力。家屬們一臉慌張地望向講台,
由於接下來的消息非常可怕,警長被巨大的壓力重重包圍。

「可是,各位先生女士們,那十三個頭顱與之前尋獲的十三
具屍體並不吻合。」

What are Monsters, Really?

I mean, what's the difference between a monster and just a regular animal?

Bear with me for a moment. Think about whales. The ancient viewed them as sea monsters, like the hydra or the leviathan. And why wouldn't they? The blue whale is the largest animal to have ever existed. Dinosaurs are seen as this giant monsters, yet none of them can hold a candle against a creature that roams our oceans at this very moment.

And how about giant squids? They were believed to be either fictitious or extinct for a long time, until a dead one showed up at a beach somewhere.

When Marco Polo first saw a rhino, he was thrilled. His conclusion upon the sight was that unicorns were real, although way uglier than in the stories. And how is a rhino less impressive than a unicorn in any way?

Take narwhals, a fan-favorite. A whale with a horn, two monsters combined into one. Yet... monsters aren't real, right? At least that's what parents say. Mine always did.

Personally, I think that hippos and rhinos and squids and tigers and elephants could all be monsters, if they weren't real animals.

怎樣才算是怪物？

我的意思是，怪物和普通動物相比，兩者有何區別？

請耐心聽我說。試想想鯨魚吧，古代人視牠們為海怪，與九頭蛇及利維坦海怪齊名。那為甚麼鯨魚是動物而不是怪物呢？藍鯨是史上最龐大的動物。就算是恐龍這種巨型陸上生物，與在浩瀚海洋裏漫遊的藍鯨相比，還是隔著遙不可及的距離。

那麼巨型魷魚又怎麼樣呢？人們一直認為牠們要麼是虛構的，要麼就已經滅絕了很長一段時間，直到它的屍體在某個地方的海灘浮現，才把這個謬誤打破。

當馬可孛羅第一次看到犀牛時，他十分激動。他對透進眼內影像的結論是：獨角獸是真實存在的！雖然長得比故事中描寫的醜陋多了。事實上，犀牛在某程度上比獨角獸更令人印象深刻吧？

以受人愛戴的獨角鯨為例吧，一頭帶角的鯨魚，一隻動物擁有兩種怪獸元素。然而，怪物都不是真實存在的……對吧？至少父母都會這樣說吧，就如我的父母也如是說。

可是我個人卻認為，如果河馬、犀牛、魷魚、老虎和大象這些動物不是真實存在的話，牠們也可能會是怪物啊。

Maybe it's not that no animals are monsters, **maybe all of them are. Or all of them can be.**

You see, a lot went through my mind as I was laying on the floor. It happened so quickly. First my arm felt funny, but I just ignored. Then, my legs stopped moving and my whole body went numb. I was paralyzed.

The first day was hard, as you can imagine.

The second was harder.

And only after three days locked inside my appartment with no food, my dog aproached me. I couldn't move. He was hungry. My cheeks must have seemed like the softer bit, because that was the first place he went.

All animals are monsters, if you push them hard enough.

又可能是,「動物不是怪物」這個觀念是錯的,而是**牠們全都是怪物,或者牠們全都可以算是怪物。**

我跟你說喔,當我躺在地板上時,我的腦袋轉個不停,浮現了很多想法。一切發生得太快了。首先是我的手臂,我覺得它有點不舒服,可是我沒有理會。接著,我的腿突然動不了,整個身體都失去知覺了。我癱瘓了。

你可以想像得到,我的第一天過得有多苦吧。

到了第二天,更是痛苦。

我被困在自己的公寓裏,在沒有糧食的情況下,只消三天,我的狗便走近了我。我無法動彈。而牠餓了。我的臉頰看起來一定是比較柔軟吧,因為這是牠第一個選擇的部分。

只要把牠們迫到絕境,所有動物都會是怪物。

The Basement

John and his wife always left notes for each other (Book club tonight, back @7:00) (Your mother called) (Need milk) on the door to the garage. It was covered in sticky notes because nobody ever threw the old ones away until they fell on the floor.

One day, John found a new note from his wife.

Honey, that stray cat I heard meowing last night is in the basement now. Can you get him? <3

John sighed. When had trespassing wildlife become his responsibility? Glancing at the basement door, he sighed again. His wife had left it cracked open, with the light on. The cat had probably already escaped. He went downstairs anyway.

It was creepy down there. Dark, dusty, and…what was that sound?

A scraping noise, whenever he took a step, like something was moving in sync with him to disguise its own movements. Cats did that. Right?

He took another step. Scrape.

流浪貓

John 和妻子習慣為彼此留下備忘錄「今晚去讀書會，七點回來」、「你媽媽打過電話來」、「要買牛奶」，並貼在通往車庫的門上。那道門被滿滿的便利貼覆蓋了，他們不會把舊的扔掉，只會任由舊的便利貼掉到地上就罷了。

有一天，John 看見了妻子寫了一張的新便利貼。

親愛的，我昨晚聽到那隻在流浪貓喵喵叫的，現在走到了地下室啊，你能幫我抓住牠嗎？<3

John 嘆了口氣。有野生動物闖入這回事，怎麼也變得要他負責呢？他瞥了一眼地下室的門，又嘆了口氣。妻子把門留了一道小縫，而且沒有關燈。那隻貓可能已經逃走了，但他還是走下了樓。

地下室這邊讓人不禁毛骨悚然。一片漆黑，加上塵土飛揚……那是甚麼聲音？

John 每踏前一步，就會同步傳來一聲刮擦的聲音，好像是故意掩飾自己的動作般。是貓兒吧，對嗎？

他又再踏前了一步。刮擦聲。

Step.

Scrape.

He stopped, almost panicking, before thinking to check his shoe. A sticky note clung to the sole, dragging when he walked. He must've stepped on it upstairs.

Honey, I called the exterminator (tomorrow @3:00) and locked the basement door. Don't go down there. I don't think that's a cat.

John looked up at the basement door; the door that had unquestionably been open when he got home, the door that, before going down the stairs, he'd shut, and presumably, inadvertently, locked behind him.

From behind the furnace, he heard a meow, but not like any cat he'd ever known. It was followed by a low chuckle.

Suddenly, John didn't think that was a cat either.

走一步。

刮擦聲。

恐慌不已的 John 停了下來，想要檢查自己的鞋子。他發現有一張便利貼黏了在鞋底，剛剛走路時一直拖行著。這張便利貼定是在樓上踩到的。

親愛的，我約了滅蟲公司（明天三點），還有，我鎖了地下室的門。不要下去那邊。我覺得那不是貓。

John 抬頭望著地下室的門——這扇門，他清楚記得，回家那時是開著的；這扇門，在他走下樓梯之前，自己親手關上的，而且很有可能不小心上鎖了。

從暖氣爐後面傳出了一聲「喵～」，但聽起來不像 John 認知的任何一隻貓。接下來 John 聽見的，是一把低沉的笑聲。

突然間，John 也覺得那不是貓了。

The Dark Night

Every child has that one thing that they are obsessed with, and Bruce was no exception. His obsession was with Batman and everything related. Friends and family all knew Batman was his thing and most of them would encourage it here and there by gifting him action figures and comic books. His parents were exceptionally supportive and would buy him video games, take him to movies and bring him to conferences where he could meet his favorite heroes.

Bruce began to become quite the collector and this only intensified his interest. He wore Batman shirts to school and he always carried his favorite action figure around.

He even started a Justice League club at school where he bestowed his friends with the titles of Superman, Wonder Woman, The Flash and others. **And at some point Bruce decided that he didn't just like Batman, he wanted to be Batman.**

He tried wearing a Batman costume to school, but the teachers made him remove the mask and cape. He started using his favorite lines and talking in what he viewed as a menacing husky voice. His parents thought it was cute and would throw birthday parties where Bruce could solve crimes, which ended with a cake celebration for the Justice League.

黑夜降臨

每個小孩都有一件讓他們非常著迷的事物，Bruce 也不例外。蝙蝠俠和其他有關蝙蝠俠的一切都讓他神魂顛倒。Bruce 的朋友和家人都知道他是蝙蝠俠的超級粉絲，他們常常會送他蝙蝠俠的人形玩偶和漫畫書。Bruce 的父母也非常支持他，會給他買電子遊戲、陪他去看電影、帶他參加可以看到他最喜歡那些英雄們的活動。

Bruce 開始成為一個小小收藏家，這也讓他愈來愈沉迷。他會穿著印有蝙蝠俠的衣服上學，而且走到哪裡也總會帶著他最喜歡的人形玩偶。

他甚至在學校開設了一個「正義聯盟俱樂部」，給朋友們頒發不同的英雄頭銜：超人、神奇女俠、閃電俠等等。**直至有一刻，Bruce 決定了他不只僅僅喜歡蝙蝠俠，他想真真正正成為蝙蝠俠。**

Bruce 試過打扮成蝙蝠俠上學，但老師要他脫下面具和斗篷；他把最愛的蝙蝠俠台詞掛在嘴邊，並用他覺得具威脅性的沙啞聲音説話。他父母認為 Bruce 這種行為很有趣，他們會在 Bruce 的生日派對上讓他「破案」，完結時會用蛋糕為「正義聯盟」慶祝。

His friends however, began to get tired of his theatrics. **Some started teasing him about it, where others tried to tell him all the reasons why he couldn't actually be Batman.**

He was determined to prove them wrong.

Things began to fall into place for Bruce that summer when his dad won the lottery and his parents decided to move to a large city. His parents were worried that Bruce would miss his friends and hometown. But to Bruce it was a dream come true. They were now rich and lived in a big city like Gotham. At his request, his dad bought him some toy gadgets to play with and his mom started taking him to a martial arts class.

But unbeknownst to them, Bruce had begun to sneak out of the house at night and wander the city streets pretending to solve crime. The area in which they lived was pretty well off, but rougher parts are never too far away in the city.

One night Bruce was caught and returned home by a police officer. The officer and his parents all had a long talk with him about the dangers of city streets at night. However, Bruce was undeterred and began only sneaking out on the darkest of nights.

然而，Bruce 的朋友開始厭倦了他的戲劇性行為，有些人開始戲弄他，**有些人則試圖勸告他，說明他無法真正成為蝙蝠俠的原因。**

可是 Bruce 非常堅定，一心想證明他們是錯的。

那年夏天，Bruce 的父親贏了彩票，父母二人決定舉家搬到大城市時，故事發展就開始變得明朗。父母擔心 Bruce 會想念朋友和家鄉，可是對 Bruce 而言，這簡直是夢想成真。Bruce 一家現在很富有，住在像葛咸城般的大城市裏。因應Bruce 的要求，父親給他買了一些玩具，而母親也帶了他去參加武術課。

可是父母不知道，Bruce 開始在晚上偷偷溜出房子，在街道上徘徊，幻想著自己在破案。他們居住的地區相當不錯，但糟糕的事總是會發生。

有一晚，Bruce 被警察抓住，然後把他送回家。警察跟他的父母整晚都在向他說教，提醒他晚上在戶外有多危險。然而，Bruce 毫不懼怕，改為在深夜才偷偷溜出去。

Tragedy struck a few months later on a dark night in October. **Bruce was always thinking about his friends back home and the reasons they said he couldn't be Batman.** There were a few that he still lacked, like the fact that he had never solved a real crime.

On that night, he was determined to finally become Batman. As he stood over his parent's bed, Bruce pulled down his mask and pulled out a knife.

在十月一個月黑風高的晚上，悲劇發生了。 Bruce 一直在想著以前的朋友，還有他們勸說自己不能成為蝙蝠俠的原因。Bruce 仍然缺乏了一些成為蝙蝠俠的元素，就像他從未真正破過案這種鐵一般的事實。

那天晚上，他決心要完完全全成為蝙蝠俠。Bruce 爬到父母的床上時，他拉下面具，亮出刀子。

The Year They Banned Porn

None of us in the industry thought that they'd actually do it – but on January 15, 2018, the government banned porn.

There was the expected outcry, but ultimately, politicians were too good at energizing the right voters while decrying the morality of the porn industry.

Work – among other things – dried up. With my savings dwindling, and the entertainment industry flooded with even more out-of-work camera jockeys like me, I started making honeymoon videos.

I'm going to ruin the ending for you now: I don't fucking make them anymore.

For those lucky enough to not know, honeymoon videos are when creeps install cameras in hotel rooms, intending to catch you fucking over your honeymoon or your beach vacation or whatever, so they can sell the videos and make money.

If you have your own equipment and a contact in the hospitality business, then the only hard part (heh) is waiting for people to travel and get laid. Sometimes you leave empty-handed, but usually not.

色情片被禁以後

業內人士都沒有想過他們真的會這樣做——2018 年 1 月 15 日，政府禁止了色情片。

雖然早已料到市民會發生強烈抗議，但始終政治家都太擅於激勵投票支持的選民，又極力譴責色情行業帶來錯誤的道德觀念。

相關的工作崗位，也隨之而乾涸了。隨著我的儲蓄減少，娛樂業界充斥著愈來愈多像我這樣的失業攝影師，我便開始製作蜜月影片。

我現在要把結局劇透了：我沒有再幹這回他媽的事了。

我要為那些不知情的幸運兒解釋一下，所謂的「蜜月影片」就是那些變態在酒店房間安裝偷拍鏡頭，在你們蜜月或海灘或其他名義的度假期間，拍下你們的歡愉片段，然後將影片出售，從中獲利。

如果你有自己的設備，而且跟酒店的人相熟，那唯一的難處（嘻嘻）就是要等待人們來旅行和上床。有時你可能會空手而回，但通常都不會。

This is how I wound up in a downtown Marriott sometime in the fall of 2018, waiting for this slip-thin little brunette and her awkward boyfriend to bang. I was chewing on a rubbery deli sandwich and playing Candy Crush on my phone when it happened.

The brunette and her date had entered the room and started fooling around. Sex all looks the same after a while – at least, in my experience – so once I saw that heavy petting was happening, I tuned them out in favor of my dinner.

A few minutes passed. I checked the camera again.

The guy and girl had been sitting on the bed, making out – but now the guy was on his back, scrambling away from the girl, his shaking, bloody hands held up pleadingly – and the rail-thin girl was stalking him slowly, her hands and face scarlet.

"What the fuck....?" I whispered to myself, unable to tear my eyes away.

I let out a half-shriek and clapped my hands over my mouth when the girl streaked towards the guy like a bullet. She buried her face into his throat, and through the grainy image I saw dark, thick liquid spray into the surrounding carpet.

2018 年秋天的某日，我待在市中心的萬豪酒店裏，緊張地等待著這個瘦弱又嬌小的棕髮女生，和她笨拙的男朋友進行魚水之歡。我邊吃著嚼不爛的三明治，邊在手機上玩著《Candy Crush》，然後事情就發生了。

他們二人進入了房間並開始鬼混著。性事其實看起來都一樣（至少憑我的經驗看來），所以每當看到他們開始熱烈地愛撫後，我就會把屏幕關掉，好讓我吃得下晚餐。

幾分鐘過去了，我再看一下攝影機。

那對男女剛剛一直坐在床上親熱，但是現在那個男的趴了在地上，極力向女生的反方向爬走，他血淋淋的雙手顫抖地舉起來哀求著甚麼，而那個乾瘦的女生正緩慢地尾隨他，她的手和臉染成通紅。

「搞甚麼鬼啊……？」我低聲對自己說，無法把視線移開。

當女孩像子彈般迅速飛奔到男孩旁邊時，我不禁驚呼了一下，並用雙手掩著嘴。透過畫面上顆粒狀的影像，我看到了她把臉埋進了他的脖子，還有一些濃稠的深色液體噴灑到地毯上。

I was suddenly and acutely aware of how quiet it was. The phone sat on the desk to my left, maddening in its implication.

I stared around the room helplessly, wishing (like a child) that somebody was there with me – if for no other reason, to corroborate what I was seeing.

On the camera's feed, I saw the girl moved away from the body. She walked to the opposite wall – the one my room shared with hers.

She turned her head to stare directly into the camera I had hidden. Lifting a bloody fist, she knocked softly, three times.

我突然強烈意識到他們的房間安靜得有多不尋常。在我左邊桌子上的電話，仿佛抓狂地暗示著要我拿起它。

我無助地張望著房間，像個孩子般在心裏冀盼會有人陪著自己──至少可以證實我所看到的一切。

我透過攝影機的屏幕，看見女孩從男孩身旁離開了。她走向對面的牆，那面連接著我房間的牆。

她轉過頭來直視我的隱藏鏡頭，然後舉起血淋淋的拳頭，輕輕敲了三下。

Be Modest and Humble

別 自 以 為 是

It's a Horrible Life

When I approach you in the park, you look pretty down-and-out. Clothes disheveled, eyes bloodshot, nose running. The holidays can be hard on people. I sit next to you on the bench, the smell of your binge-drinking invading my nostrils.

"How're you doing, friend?" I ask gently.

"Not so good," you reply. "I got fired from my job. Can you believe that? Fired so close to Christmas. My girlfriend keeps saying we're going to get evicted if I don't find something soon. Doesn't she think I know that? I reached out to my friends but none of them will help me because I've asked so many times before. You know, sometimes I think everyone would be better off if I was never born."

You look shocked, as if you can't believe you unloaded so much on a total stranger. **I'm familiar with this effect I have on people.**

"Now, I'm sure that's not true," I say. "Listen, you might not believe this, but I'm an angel sent from Heaven to watch over people like you. Why don't I show you what it would be like if you were never born? Then you can see how much everyone needs you."

You sniffle. "Okay."

悲劇人生

那時我在公園長椅靠近你，你看起來很落魄——衣衫凌亂、眼睛滿布血絲、鼻水流個不停。假期對有些人來說可是很痛苦的。我坐到你旁邊，強烈的酒氣馬上竄進我的鼻孔。

「嘿，你還好嗎？」我溫柔地問。

「不太好。」你回答：「我被解僱了，快到聖誕節了還解僱我，你說是不是很離譜？我女朋友常常嘮叨，說這樣下去我們會被房東趕走的，不用她說我也知道啦，可是我真的找不到工作啊……我試過向朋友求助，但因為我之前已經問過他們太多次了，他們現在都不願意幫我了。有時我覺得如果我從未出生過，每個人都會變得更好，你明白嗎？」

你對於自己竟然對一個陌生人大吐苦水感到驚訝，露出難以置信的表情。**我卻很習慣其他人對我會有這種反應。**

「不要這樣想吧。」我說：「聽好了，你可能不會相信，可我是從天堂下凡的天使，專門看顧像你這樣的人。不如我讓你看看，要是你沒有出生的話，世界會變得怎麼樣？看完之後你就會知道大家原來很需要你。」

你抽抽鼻子道：「好吧。」

I produce a tiny bell from my pocket and ring it. Suddenly, we're in front of a magnificent mansion.

"Where are we?" you ask.
"I took you to your girlfriend. Let's see how sad she is without you."

We peek in the window at the impressive interior with expensive furnishings. Your girlfriend is at the dinner table with an exceedingly handsome man, holding his hand. She laughs at something he says and strokes the hair of a beautiful child sitting next to her.

"But... she's better off without me!" you exclaim, horrified.
"Oh, I'm so sorry," I say. "Let's try someone else."

I ring my bell and we're at your parents' house. A young man who bears a resemblance to you walks outside.

"Is that... my brother? But it can't be. He died years ago."
"If I had to guess," I offer. "He may be alive because you weren't around to influence him to drive so fast."

我從口袋掏出一個小鈴鐺，然後敲響它。下一秒，我們就在一座宏偉的豪宅前。

「這裏是甚麼地方？」你問道。
「我帶你去見你的女朋友。讓我們看看，在沒有你的世界裏，她會有多難過。」

我們從窗口瞥進去，看到裏面金碧輝煌的裝潢，也放滿了名貴的家具。你的女朋友和一位俊朗非凡的男子一同坐在餐桌旁，還牽著對方的手。他跟她說了些甚麼，她聽罷便開朗大笑起來，並撫摸著坐在她旁邊，那個漂亮孩子的頭髮。

「可是…她沒有我還活得比較好啊！？」你惶恐地驚呼道。
「噢，我很抱歉。」我說：「試試看其他人吧。」

我敲響了鈴鐺，然後我們就到了你父母家。有個看起來有點像你的年輕人走到屋子外面。

「那是……我的哥哥嗎？不可能啊？他早在很多年前就過世了啊。」
「要是讓我猜的話……」我主動提出：「應該是因為沒有你在身邊叫他駛快點，所以他還活著吧。」

I watch your face as your parents come out of the house, smiling and hugging your brother in a way they never hugged you.

"Oh God," you say. "Take me back. Please. I can't stand another second here."

I ring the bell and we're back in a world that you know is worse because of your existence. You run away and I wonder how you're going to do it: pills, a gun, or maybe jumping off a tall bridge.

I know you won't be able to live with what I've shown you; no one has ever been able to.

None of it was real, of course. But you think it is. And that's enough.

I remove my hat to give my horns some air and keep walking, looking for the next poor soul depressed during this fine holiday season.

你的父母從屋子裏走出來，微笑著擁抱你的哥哥，他們從來不會這樣熱切對待你。我看著你臉上的表情變化。

「天啊……」你開口：「拜託你帶我回去，我不想在這裏再多待一秒。」

我再次敲響了鈴鐺，我們便回到這個因有你存在而變得更壞的世界。你跑走了。我很好奇你會選擇以下哪種方法：服藥、吞槍，還是從高橋跳下去？

我知道你看完我展示的那些片段後都不想再活了，因為每個人都是這樣，你也不例外。

當然，那些畫面全都是假的。可是你卻深信不疑，這樣就足夠了。

我脫掉帽子，讓我的角好好呼吸一下，然後繼續踱步，在這個美好的假日期間，尋找下一個沮喪的可憐靈魂。

Dances With Sixteen Devils

A loud, harsh impact.

Then a long dream.

I awoke in a suit in the middle of a ballroom. Black and white tiles stretched beneath my expensive shoes, running to red velvet curtains.

Before me stood an array of men and women, lined up neatly and waiting patiently. I sensed their oppressive energy, yet I walked up to the first dancer, whose hand extended towards me seemed so threatening when paired with his saccharine smile. I took his hand, the small gesture allowing me the knowledge of his name.

The music started, and we danced.

As I and *Guilt* spun, he choked me, displaying friends and family, the arts that would die without my hand to spawn them. He handed me over to *Shame*.

Shame tittered lightly, sparking a sense of nakedness and vulnerability beyond the likes of which I'd ever known- before the next handoff.

I soon found myself in *Regret*'s strong arms, and he spun me

與十六位惡魔共舞

一股震耳欲聾的衝擊。

接著是一段漫長的夢。

我醒來發現自己穿著禮服，身處舞廳中間。我穿著昂貴的鞋子，踏著黑白相間的瓷磚，放眼望去，舞廳兩旁是紅色的天鵝絨窗簾。

在我面前站了排列整齊的男男女女，正耐心等待著。我感覺到他們壓抑的能量，但我還是走向了第一位舞者。他伸手向我，配以他甜得過分的微笑，使我覺得他似乎很有威脅性。我握住他的手，他作了個小手勢讓我知道他的名字。

音樂響起了，我們便翩翩起舞。

當我和*內疚*轉著圈時，他掐著我的脖子，向我展示失去了我的朋友和家人，就如失去了靈感的藝術品。然後他把我交給了*羞恥*。

*羞恥*暗暗地竊笑著，向我引發了一種從未感到這般難受的赤裸感和脆弱感後，又把我交到下一位舞者手上。

我很快就發現自己落入了*後悔*強壯的臂彎中，他使勁地帶著

so forcefully that I longed for a way to turn back time. It was almost crippling.

Next, *Obligation* reminded me of appointments, of schoolworks, of meet-ups with friends. I began to sense a familiar panic. What if I missed everything because I wasted so much time dancing?

I tried to flee, but *Irritability* swooped in, not failing to remind me how annoying the previous dancer could be. How persistent she was. And like that, the next dancer had me.

Melancholy burdened me, knowing how well *Obligation* had worn me out, and suddenly everything she described felt more like chains weighing me, trapping me, hopelessly.

Exhaustion and I dragged ourselves along together, unenthused. Him due to his nature, and I due to the chains now encircling my ankles. It took much effort for him to pass me on.

Lethargy and I moved at a snail's pace, our movements a mockery of the term "dancing". The music slowed and lowered in tone. My lack of motivation meant I could barely make it to the next waiting dancer.

As though to torture me, the music suddenly revived, and

我轉圈，以致我恨不得找到扭轉時間的方法。我快要跛腳了。

接下來，*責任*讓我想起了學校作業、預約，還有朋友聚會。我開始感覺到一陣熟悉的恐慌。要是我只顧跳舞，浪費了那麼多時間，而錯過了一切的話，我該怎麼辦？

我試圖逃跑，但是*暴怒*突然撲向我，提醒著我前一位舞者有多惱人，有多麼固執。就這樣，下一位舞者抓住了我。

*憂鬱*使我感到沉重，雖然知道*責任*讓我疲憊不堪，可是突然之間，她所描述的一切，感覺更像是枷鎖般使我背負重擔，同時絕望地困住了我。

*疲憊*和我同樣失去熱情地拖著腿。他會這樣做，是基於自己的本性，而我只是因為現在腳踝上綁著了鏈子。他花了很大的力氣才能鬆手把我送走。

*慵懶*和我以蝸牛的速度擺動著，我們的動作可說是對「跳舞」一詞的嘲弄。音樂慢了下來，也降低了音調。我缺乏動力，使我幾乎無法把自己帶到下一位舞者的手中。

像是要折磨我般，音樂突然回復激昂了，*失眠*狂暴地喚醒著我，迫使我保持警覺。

Sleeplessness whisked me about in a frenzy, forcing alertness on me.

I was awake enough to listen with distress as *Distorted Self-Image* cruelly whispered into my ear.

Self-Hatred piggybacked off the prior dancer's words.

Self-Harm Contemplation teased me, holding a blade before me, seeing if I would take it.

Suicidal Ideation regaled to me my most distinctive suicidal fantasies.

Isolation subtly swept me away from the other dancers, and yet further still from those who wanted to help me. The music faded. Then it was gone.

Left with *Silence*, who sewed my mouth shut and insisted my problems didn't matter, I was finally ready.

The final dancer, *Death*, offered wide open arms, and I approached. Fast.

Too fast. I tripped.

*扭曲的自我形象*殘忍地向我耳語時，我清醒得很，被迫聽著一切悲痛的描述。

*自我仇恨*背負著前一位舞者的話語。

*自殘沉思*嘲笑我，在我面前拿著一把刀片，試探著我是否會接過它。

*自殺意念*向我講述了一些最獨特的自殺幻想。

*孤立*巧妙地把我帶離了其他舞者，而且對那些想要幫助我的人還要更遠離一些。我漸漸聽不見音樂，然後它就消失了。

剩下*沉默*在我面前，它把我的嘴縫了起來，讓我閉嘴，並堅持我的問題無關緊要，堅持説我終於準備好了。

最後的舞者，是*死亡*，他張開雙臂，我很快便靠近了他。

太快了。我絆倒了。

I fell. I woke.

In the hospital room, my family and friends rejoiced at my awakening. I had nothing to rejoice. At the window, the final dancer still stood, waiting. He mouthed something before vanishing.

"Next year."

我跌倒了。我醒了。

在病房裏，家人和朋友都因為我甦醒過來而感到欣喜，卻沒有甚麼事讓我值得高興的。望向窗外，我看見最後的舞者仍然站著、等待著。他在消失之前說了句話——

「明年吧。」

Gaslight

Dear Dave,

I never thought anyone could be so despicable, not even you. And don't try to make me think I'm crazy like you did when we were married. You're the one who's crazy.

I know that now. **You'd have to be, to do something like this.**

I haven't contacted the police. I don't think either of us wants them involved after what happened before. Instead, I'm going to put everything into this email, as a permanent record of your actions.

As per the agreement, you were to drop off our daughter at my apartment on Friday. At first everything appeared to be fine. She seemed like the same old Becky—hair in braids like I used to fix it, goofy smile, and that ratty Hello Kitty pillow she carries everywhere.

But after you drove away, she seemed different somehow—nervous, frightened--like someone I didn't recognize. **Not like my Becky at all.**

That's when I understood what you'd done.Did you really think I wouldn't know? I'm her mother, you bastard.

假面人

親愛的 Dave：

我從未想過原來有人可以如此卑鄙，更加沒想過那會是你。別把我想得跟結婚那時的你一樣瘋狂。

你才是瘋子，我現在領教了。**要不是你的腦袋壞掉了，怎會做出這樣的事？**

我還沒有報警喔，我相信你跟我一樣，都不想他們介入之前發生的事吧。我將把所有內容都打在這封電子郵件，讓你所做的一切都可以永久記錄下來。

按照協議，逢星期五你都要把女兒送回我的公寓。起初一切似乎都很順利。她看起來跟以前的 Becky 很像，梳著像我幫她綁的辮子，掛著傻傻的笑容，還帶著 Becky 到哪裏也帶著，那個破舊的 Hello Kitty 枕頭。

但是在你開車離開之後，她似乎有所變化，會變得緊張和害怕，這感覺很陌生。**這樣的她一點都不像我的 Becky。**

那時我才明白你做了甚麼。你真的覺得我會甚麼都不知道嗎？我可是她的媽媽啊，你這個混蛋！

She tried to cover for you. She denied that anything was wrong. But I thought of a way to find out the truth. I took her for a ride in the boat, out past the reef, where we used to go fishing as a family. Remember? It's so nice and peaceful out there, perfect for talking, but we just sat quietly, watching the stars.

Then I pushed her into the water.

Ha! Who's the crazy one now, Dave? Did you actually think you could fool me? You really thought I'd believe that she was my daughter, my Becky? Sure, she looked like her, talked and cried like her, even wore her clothes, with "Becky" written on the tags.

But you forgot one thing: our daughter knows how to swim.

That imposter, that phony Becky you sent, oh, she pretended she could swim. She even followed the boat for a few hours. But eventually she went under, just like the big fat dirty faker that she was. Even with her last breath, she was still calling me mama, still pretending to be my Becky!

Can you imagine? She was a filthy little liar liar pants on fire. Just like you, Dave.

她試圖替你辯護，堅稱沒有甚麼不對勁。但我想到了找出真相的方法——我帶她坐船出海，到礁石後面那邊，我們以前常常在那裏釣魚的啊，你還記得嗎？那裏舒適又安靜，是個談心的好地方。但我們只是靜靜坐著，抬頭看星。

然後我把她推到海裏。

哈！Dave，現在誰是瘋子啊？你真的以為可以騙得到我嗎？以為我會相信她是我的女兒、我親愛的 Becky 嗎？她的確長得很像 Becky，連説話和哭鬧也學得很像，甚至還穿著她那些標籤上寫著「Becky」的衣服。

但是你忘了一件事：我們的女兒會游泳啊。

你帶過來那個假到不行的冒牌貨 Becky，哼，她裝作會游泳呢！她甚至尾隨著小船游了好幾個小時，但最終她還是沉了下去，活該她這個又髒又賤的假人。就算只剩下最後一口氣，她還是叫我做媽媽，還是繼續假扮是我的 Becky！

你能想像她有多誇張嗎？Dave，這個假面人跟你一樣是滿口謊言的臭騙子！

This was supposed to be my weekend. My time. The doctors said I was ready. The judge agreed. You were the only one who still thought I was unstable. But you were wrong, weren't you? Last chance, Dave. Bring Becky over here now. The real Becky this time.

Sincerely,
Laura

這本應是屬於我的周末，我的歡樂時光，現在被她毀了。那些醫生說我準備好了，法官也同意了，只有你還在認為我情況不穩定。可你真是大錯特錯了啊。Dave，我給你最後一次機會，立刻把 Becky 帶過來，我是說真的那個 Becky 喔。

Laura 敬上

Life of a Traitor

You know, it's funny really. In a maximum-security prison, filled with murderers and rapists, the worst thing they can do to you is leave you completely alone. Solitary confinement.

The human brain needs input, or it quickly descends into horrifying madness of its own company.

In 2086 when the world government fell into a dictatorship, capital punishment became very common. However, it was solitary confinement that people feared. That was reserved just for treason.

I spent my working life making the solitary confinement cells and carrying out the confinement. Here's how it works.

The cells are molded to exactly fit the condemned. They are human shaped coffins. Arms out to the side at 30°, legs 45° apart. For the insertion process the traitors are sedated.

The eyes, ears and mouth are not damaged, but all are sealed permanently shut. An automated breathing tube inserted through the throat. Three IV lines are inserted to feed nutrients; we use three lines in case of mechanical failure on

叛徒的餘生

你知道嗎？這回事很有趣呢。在一所滿是殺人犯和強姦犯的最高警備監獄裏，他們對你最苛刻的待遇，就是讓你完全被孤立，也就是單獨監禁。

人類的大腦需要資訊的刺激，否則很快就會因沒有刺激而陷入可怕的神經錯亂。

2086 年，世界政府陷入了獨裁統治，死刑變得非常普遍。然而，令人們懼怕的是單獨監禁，所以那只用來懲罰叛國罪的犯人。

我整個工作生涯都花在製作單獨監禁的囚室，並對犯人執行關押，以下是它的構造和懲罰原理。

囚室是根據被判刑的死囚而度身訂造的，可說是個人形棺材。雙臂向外張開三十度，雙腿之間分開四十五度。死囚會先被注射鎮靜劑，才安置到囚室之中。

我們不會弄傷死囚的眼睛、耳朵和嘴巴，但三者都會被永久封閉。經喉嚨插入一條自動呼吸管，另外再插入三條靜脈導管來餵養養分。以防其中一條導管發生故障，所以我們用了

one. Catheters are inserted to handle waste.

The condemned are sealed in and buried in the very public, traitors' graveyard. With enough autonomous supplies to last 80 years, but to be considered dead from that day.

Nasty right?

Well that has been my job for the last 20 years, and I am pretty numb to the idea of it. One person a day entered the traitors' graveyard. This was so that the condemned persons story could feature on the evening news. Along with their frenzied begging for a pardon. It hasn't caused me distress in many years.

That was until last week, when I was convicted of treason.

I can't really argue, I'm guilty. But after seeing the things I have seen, is it surprising I turned to murder. This regime needs to be brought down, this barbaric practice of solitary confinement needs to end now!

But it will take a better man than me to achieve that.

三條導管。亦有插入導尿管以處理排泄物。

安置好死囚後，他們會被密封起來，並埋在公開的叛徒墓園。雖然囚室供應的養分可以供他們維生八十年，但從下葬那天起，死囚就會被視為死去了。

聽起來很嚇人對吧？

那是我過去二十年的工作，我對這個概念已經頗麻木了。每天都有一個死囚被埋葬到叛徒墓園，到了晚間新聞時段，電視台就可以報道，有關當天被判刑那個死囚的故事了。雖然每天也聽見他們發瘋似的在乞求我們赦免他們的罪，可是多年來我也沒有感到很困擾。

直到上週，我被判犯了叛國罪。

我無法爭辯，因為我的確是犯了罪。當我親眼目擊過一切事情之後，我會變成殺人犯其實也不足為奇。我們要打倒這個政權，要立即結束單獨監禁這種野蠻行為！

不過，要實現這個目標的話，就需要一個比我更好的人。

Today I woke up from the sedation. My eyes and mouth sealed shut. Deafening silence and dazzling blackness greet my panicked brain. Fight or flight response kicks in and I choose between 0 options.

I can't move an inch, even my fingers are molded in place.

I just keep thinking about all those people I put down here, all the things I wish I had done differently.

I can't have been down here for more than a week and I would choose death if I could.

I would give anything to take back the treason I committed. The 7,000 people I killed.

I only did it to save others from untold suffering.

I did it while they were sedated. A syringe of air into their veins to cause cardiac arrest. One murder each day for 20 years.

It's just me alive down here, living the life of a traitor.

今天，我從鎮靜狀態中醒來，眼睛和嘴巴被密封起來了。震耳欲聾的沉默和耀眼的黑暗正跟我那陷入恐慌的大腦問好。被大腦激起「戰鬥或逃跑」反應的我，有無限個空白的選擇。

我完全動彈不得，連手指也被固定住了。

我不斷想起在這裏被我處決的所有人，後悔著自己做過的所有事情。

在這裏待一個星期已經是我的極限了，如果可以的話，我想快點死去。

我甘願付出一切來撤消我犯下的叛國罪，也希望自己沒有殺掉那七千個人。

我只是為了拯救他們，免除他們受無盡的苦難才會這樣做。

我趁他們在鎮靜狀態時才動手的——把空氣注射到靜脈，以致心臟驟停。每天都殺一個人，二十年來，天天如是。

現在只有我活生生的在這裏，餘生過著叛徒應得的生活。

My Girlfriend was Always Afraid of Being Alone

From an early age, she always felt like something was off whenever no one else was in the room. It's a bit strange, sure, but I love her, so I don't care.

Whenever she was afraid, my girl would call and I'd go running. "My hero" she'd say. Eventually it seemed to make more sense to move in together, as I was already spending most of my days at her place. So that's what we did. Those were the happiest days of my life.

Lately, though, she's been acting a lot stranger than normal. This one time we were in the living room and, out of nowhere, she starts screaming. Also, she's been waking up in the middle of the night, shivering, crying on my arms. Once she dropped a plate on the floor when I offered help with dinner, and proceeded to lock herself in the room for the rest of the night.

Yeah, she's been acting strange alright, but who am I to judge? It doesn't matter if she cries at night sometimes. **And it doesn't matter that's been almost three months since the doctors pulled the plug, after it was clear I wouldn't recover from the car accident.** She is afraid of being alone. She needs me.

I'll never leave my girl alone again.

長伴身旁

我女朋友從小以來，只要身處的房間裏沒有其他人，她就總會覺得哪裏不妥。這聽起來的確是有點奇怪，可是我愛她，所以我不在乎這點小事。

每當她害怕時，她都會打電話給我，我每次都會不顧一切的跑到她身邊陪伴著她。「你是我的英雄。」她會這樣對我說。我們最後覺得搬到一起住似乎更好，反正我大部分時間都待在她的家。所以我們就一起生活啦，那段時間是我一生中最幸福的日子。

然而，最近她變得很奇怪。就像有一次我們在客廳，她突然尖叫起來。此外，她經常在半夜醒過來，身體顫抖著，在我懷裏哭泣。又有一次，當我跟她一起準備晚餐時，她突然把盤子丟了地上，然後把自己鎖在房間，整晚再沒有出來。

是的，她變得很奇怪，可是我有甚麼資格批判她呢？她有時會在夜裏哭泣，那沒有關係。**眼看我不會從車禍中恢復過來，於是醫生拔掉了插頭，到現在已經差不多三個月了，**那也沒有關係。因為她害怕獨處，她需要我。

我絕不會再讓我親愛的女孩苦無依靠的。

5070

I'm no claustrophobic. However, I'm a very curious individual. Curious to a dangerous degree, claims my husband.

This is why I locked the bathroom door. He'd naturally panic if he witnessed me attempting to fit myself inside a small cabinet, just for the sake of seeing if I could.

But of course, I'd casually pondered about the possibility for as long as we'd lived in the house, given I was more on the petite side. For no particular reason except to quell any uncertainty regarding the issue, I ascertained that myself and the cabinet were alone together. No interruptions.

Observing the dimensions of the cabinet, I contemplated how to best insert myself. A few awkward attempts later, and I was mostly inside. The door hadn't closed in its entirety, much to my frustration.

I squirmed around in annoyance, before taking a few moments to recompose myself. After that, I identified the obstacle: my hip, protruding slightly from the threshold. **A slight adjustment allowed the door to close with a satisfying thud.**

5070立方英吋

我不是幽閉恐懼症患者。但是我是個充滿好奇心的人。丈夫形容我是「好奇到一個危險的程度」。

這就是我鎖上浴室門的原因。如果他親眼目睹我只是因為好奇，而試圖把自己塞進一個小櫃子裏，他肯定會嚇壞了。

可是，只要我們還住在這間房子裏，而且我算是比較嬌小的，好奇的我就會偶然地想著「把自己塞進小櫃子」的可能性。除了想滿足自己的好奇心外，我沒有其他特別的理由，我只是想確保自己能和小櫃子單獨相處，而且不會有任何干擾。

我邊觀察著小櫃子的尺寸，邊深思著如何能把自己完美地塞進去。經過幾次笨拙的嘗試後，明明我的身體大部分都在櫃裏了，可是櫃門卻無法全部關上，這讓我非常沮喪。

我懊惱地扭來扭去，過了一會才回復冷靜。然後，我認清了讓我關不了門的障礙物：我的臀部，稍稍突出了櫃門一點兒。輕微的調整後，**櫃門發出了讓人覺得滿足的關門聲。**

Reveling in my victory for about three seconds, I realized exactly how uncomfortable the position was, and moved to let myself out. Suddenly, the door was not budging.

No big deal, I figured. It's a pretty dated bathroom. Paint probably made the door stick or something. I bumped the door with my hip a bit harder, only for it to remain firmly shut. I breathed a bit faster, remembering the locked bathroom door.

I elbowed the stubborn thing, noting that it felt more like something was sitting, leant up against the door, preventing my escape. I thrashed as best I could in the confined space to no avail. The light wooden thing seemed akin to concrete then. I screamed for help, despite the low probability that my husband would hear me. Perhaps it was panic. Perhaps it was unprecedented fear...

...I passed out.

When I came to, I was lying on the cold bathroom tile, my husband hovering over me with a highly concerned expression. "That was a dangerous stunt you pulled," he lectured sternly. "**Locking the bathroom door?** What were you thinking? Look what I did in order to come save you." He gestured to the door, its lock now broken.

陶醉在成功感的我，大約三秒鐘後，便意識到這個姿勢原來是多麼不舒服，而且想動身離開了。可是，門一動也不動。

沒甚麼大不了的，我心想。這是一個相當陳舊的浴室，可能是油漆黏住了櫃門或甚麼的。我稍為用力地用臀部撞向櫃門，然而它還是那麼「堅定不移」。我想起上了鎖的浴室門，呼吸不禁變得急促起來。

我用手肘擊向頑固的櫃門，此刻我才注意到，像是有甚麼東西坐在小櫃子前，並靠在門上，不讓我逃脫。我盡可能在這個密閉空間中劇烈扭動著，卻完全無濟於事。這個輕木製的櫃此刻仿佛變成了混凝土製般。儘管丈夫不太可能聽到，但我還是尖聲呼救著。也許因為驚慌失措，也許因為前所未有的恐懼……

……總之我昏過去了。

當我醒過來的時候，我正躺在浴室冰冷的瓷磚上，丈夫用擔心得要命的表情俯視著我。「你剛剛『表演』的是很危險的特技啊。」他嚴厲地說：「**鎖上浴室門**？你腦袋到底在想甚麼？你看看我為了救你做了些甚麼！」他指著門，門鎖現在變得破破爛爛了。

"At least we can get a new one now, like you wanted."

He couldn't help but crack a grin at this. "You're insane."

"It's why you married me."
"Yeah. But seriously... you could've suffocated. Never do anything like that again."

I swore not to. I filled the thing with as many damned towels as I could find. Beforehand, I examined the door closely, trying to figure out what went wrong. Not sticky paint. Not a malfunctioning hinge. Not a faulty lock or handle, either.

The cabinet door possessed neither.

「至少現在可以換一個新的啊，如你所願了啊。」

他忍不住笑了起來：「你真是個瘋子。」

「不然你怎麼會把我娶回家？」
「對啊。但是說真的，你可能會因此窒息的啊，你不要再那樣做了。」

我發誓我不會再這樣做了。接著，我找來了很多該死的毛巾，把它們通通塞滿了櫃子。不過在那之前，我仔細檢查了櫃門，嘗試弄清楚到底是哪裏出了問題。沒有黏黏的油漆，鉸鏈沒有故障，鎖和門把也沒有故障。

櫃門也沒有被鬼附身。

The Thing About Lake Emily

The first time I ever lied to my wife was on our honeymoon. We were at Lake Emily, where she'd spent all her childhood summers, the place she loved most in the world.

One evening, we borrowed a boat from our hotel and went out to watch the sunset, maybe skinny-dip if nobody was around.

God, she was beautiful, my wife, wearing her favorite red dress, her skin glowing in the light of the setting sun. I remember thinking I was the luckiest man alive.

"Did I ever tell you about Emily?" she asked, trailing her hand in the water. "She drowned here, years ago. Her long hair got caught in seaweed while she was swimming. Nobody noticed she was gone. They found her the next day, floating upside down, her feet just inches from the surface, her hair still tangled in the weeds."

"Jesus."

"She haunts this lake," continued my wife, clearly enjoying scaring me. "Grandma always said, 'Tie your hair back when you swim or Emily will grab it and pull you down.'"

艾米麗湖的秘密

我第一次向妻子撒謊，是在度蜜月的時候。我們當時在艾米麗湖，她小時候每逢夏天都會到這裏消遣，艾米麗湖是她在這世界上最喜歡的地方。

有天晚上，我們向酒店借了一艘船，到外面看日落，如果沒有人在附近的話，我們可能會裸泳吧。

天啊，妻子穿起她最喜歡的紅色連身裙，皮膚在夕陽的照耀下閃閃發亮，她真的很美。我記得那時我覺得自己是世上最幸運的人。

「我有告訴過你關於艾米麗湖的事嗎？」她用手撥著水問道：「多年前有個名叫 Emily 的女生在這裏淹死了。她游泳時，長髮被海藻纏住了。可是沒有人注意到她不見了。人們第二天才發現她，屍體頭向下的浮了起來，她的腳離水面只有幾英吋，頭髮還是跟海藻糾結在一起。」

「天啊。」
「她還冤魂不散地逗留在這個湖，」妻子續說道，顯然很享受嚇唬著我。「我奶奶總是這麼說：『下水前記得把頭髮綁起來，否則 Emily 會抓住你的頭髮，然後把你拉到水底。』」

"Great spot for a honeymoon," I said.

She laughed.

"It's just a ghost story. C'mon, let's swim."
"Now?" I glanced at the water. It seemed dark and oily, boiling with seaweed. "Here?"

"I always take precautions," **said my wife, holding up her braid, tied tightly with a red ribbon that matched her dress.** "Besides, I love this place. Nothing can hurt me here."

She took off her clothes, and dove in.

Seconds later, she struggled into the boat, gasping for air.

"Something grabbed my hair," she whispered.

I thought she was joking, but the fear in her eyes was real. I wrapped a towel around her, and held her as she stared at the water.

Then she laughed.

「這真是個度蜜月的好地方呢⋯⋯」我説。

她笑了。

「只是個鬼故事而已嘛,來吧,我們游泳吧。」
「現在?」我瞥了一眼湖水,可是水看起來又黑又油油的,而且滿滿都是海藻。「這裏?」

「我向來也是未雨綢繆的人呢。」妻子説罷便抓起她的辮子,**用一條與她的衣服相配的紅絲帶,緊緊的綁了起來。**「而且,我很愛這個地方嘛,這裏沒甚麼可以傷到我的。」

她脱掉衣服,接著潛入水中。

幾十秒鐘之後,她艱難地猛游回來上船,氣喘吁吁的。

「有東西抓住了我的頭髮。」她低聲説。

我以為她在開玩笑,但她眼中流露出的恐懼倒是真的。我用毛巾裹著她,然後抱著一直盯著水面的她。

接著她笑了起來。

"I'm so ridiculous," she said, shaking out her hair. "I scared myself with that silly story. It was my imagination. I love this place."

I nodded, but I just wanted to get the hell out of there. I started pulling up the anchor.

"Nothing can ever hurt me here," she added.
"Of course not," I said.

A lie.

Because when the anchor came out of the water, **I saw my wife's red hair ribbon, tied around it in a neat little bow.**

「我太可笑了。」她甩著頭髮説著：「竟然讓這個愚蠢的故事嚇壞了自己，那明明只是我的幻想而已。我很愛這個地方的呢。」

我點點頭，但我只想快點離開那裡。我開始把錨拉起來。

「這裏沒有甚麼可以傷到我的。」她補充道。
「當然沒有。」我回應。

那是謊話。

因為當錨露出水面那時，**我看到了錨上有個綁得很整齊的小蝴蝶結，那是妻子用來綁頭髮的紅絲帶。**

A Twin Thing

Listen. I'm not a serial killer. This is a one-off thing.Christ alive. Shut up. Just, fucking lay there and keep quiet. I'm trying to concentrate. This is my first time and I'm trying to get it right.

So. First off, I'm really sorry about all this. Second, I'm going to be babbling for a little while. Nerves. So sorry about that too.

Me and my twin brother were born like 20 seconds apart. We were practically joined at the hip from birth all the way up to high school. But then, something switched inside us and we went out of our way to be different. He sort of went his way and I went mine.

Shit, you know how it is at that age. Rebelling against expectations and trying to find yourself and all that.

God damn it, where the fuck is the... okay, if I was a blowtorch where would I be... this is gonna sound stupid, and I apologize if it makes it weird, but can you see a blowtorch anywhere in this room? It's supposed to be... ah, there it is. The tool table was blocking it.

So as I said, he went his way and I went mine. But we always had this connection, you know? It's a twin thing. I can usually

雙胞胎才懂的事

聽好了。我不是連環殺手。這只是一次性的事情。老天啊，給我閉嘴，給我他媽的躺在那裏不要作聲。我正在集中精神。因為這是我的第一次，我努力讓自己不要出錯。

好吧。首先，我對這一切真的深感抱歉。其次，我接下來會嘮叨一會兒，神經緊張嘛，我對此也很抱歉呢。

我和雙胞胎哥哥的出生時間只相隔二十秒。從出生到高中以來，我們一直友好得如膠似漆。可是後來，我們的內心產生了一些變化，我們竭盡全力想把自己變得跟對方有所不同，於是我們各走各路。

媽的，你知道那個年紀就是那樣的嘛。別人對自己有甚麼期望都不會遵從，只顧追尋自我，或者諸如此類的反叛行為。

該死的，到哪裏去了啊？好吧，如果我是一個噴槍，我會在哪裏……這聽起來很笨，如果你覺得很奇怪的話，我為此道歉，但是你看到噴槍在房間的哪個位置嗎？應該在……啊，找到了。工具枱擋住了它。

像我之前說的，我們各走各路。但我們之間總是有著一種聯繫，你知道嗎？這是雙胞胎才懂的事。我通常都能知道他的感受。我們有點像……互相體驗著各自的經歷，特別是當我

tell what he's feeling. We sort of... pick up experiences from each other. Especially when emotions are running high. I remember one time when we were kids, he slipped and broke his wrist... that hurt me like hell. I was fine, but the pain was just radiating up my forearm.

All kinds of things. Heh. The night I popped my cherry he told me he... ahem.

Anyway. He helped me out recently. I mean, he *really* stepped up. Me and the Missus broke up and I couldn't stay at home anymore. He let me crash at his place. Helped get my shit together. Helped me find an apartment. Even paid the security deposit for me. He had my back when it mattered.

And... he's in the hospital this week. Throat cancer; he doesn't even smoke, how fucking unlucky is that? His operation is tomorrow. He's worried bad. I can tell. This very second, he's listening to music trying hard not to think about it. *God*, how I hate Kelly Clarkson.

He's jonesing for his usual fix but he can't go out and do it himself. I owe him.

Like I said, *I'm* not a serial killer. This is a one-off thing. A twin thing. You understand.

們情緒高漲的時候，感受尤其深刻。我記得有一次，當我們還是小孩的時候，他滑倒並摔斷了手腕，我痛得快死掉了。我絲毫無傷，可是痛感更由手腕一直蔓延到前臂。

還有其他各種各樣的事情吧，嘿。我初夜的那晚，他告訴我他……咳咳。

怎樣也好，總之他最近幫了我很多。我的意思是，他*真的*進步了不少。我和妻子鬧翻了，所以我不能待在家了。他不但讓我到他的家過夜，替我收拾殘局，也替我找了一間公寓，甚至還為我付了按金。到了重要關頭，他總會替我撐腰。

可是……他今個星期住進了醫院。咽喉癌──他明明不抽煙，為何會這麼該死的不幸呢？他明天就要動手術了。我看得出來，他擔心得要命。此時此刻，他聽著音樂，努力讓自己不去想手術的事。*天啊*，我是多麼討厭 Kelly Clarkson。

他很想去辦那些恆常要處理的事情，但他無法外出，便不能親自處理了。這是我欠他的。

就如我說的，*我*不是連環殺手。這只是一次性的事情。這是雙胞胎才懂的事。你也該懂的。

The Gatekeeper

As the tsunami of darkness washes over you, extinguishing the light in each and every neuron. As your heart runs out of time and you gasp your last mortal breath.

As you Die.

You meet a figure who gives you a terrible choice.

Somehow, as though burnt into your brain, is this figures name *The Gatekeeper*.

A tall thin authoritative presence, very slightly bowed down from the weight of the burden it carries.

Though *The Gatekeeper*'s features are somehow elusive, you can sense just how old the time withered soul that stands before you is.

The Gatekeeper explains that you are one of only a small number of original humans. This small group are given the following choice every time they die. No tricks, no traps, just a terrible choice.

You can be reincarnated, or you can be remembered for the life you have just lived.

看門人

當一股黑暗的海嘯向你襲來、每一個神經元中的光熄滅之時；
當你的心臟已油盡燈枯；當你喘息著在生的最後一口氣之時；

當你死去之時。

你會遇到一個給你可怕選擇的人物。

不知何故，這個人物的名字——*看門人*，仿佛早已烙在你的
大腦般。

高瘦又具權威性的它，因背負重擔而墜得微微曲著身子。

雖然*看門人*的特徵有點難以捉摸，但你也可以感覺到，在你
面前的這個靈魂，已被時間磨蝕多久了。

*看門人*解釋說，你是少數原始人類中的一員。這群人每次死
亡時都可以有以下選擇。沒有欺騙成分，也不是陷阱，只是
一個可怕的選擇。

你可以選擇轉世，或者你可以選擇被人們記住你剛剛活過的
一生。

If you choose to be reincarnated, then all memory and all traces of your last life will be wiped from the earth. Your children will become children of other men and women. Your partner will have lived a solitary life or Loved another. Your accomplishments and your faults, all spread around to other humans. The life you have just finished living will never have happened. You will be born again. A new human, somewhere in the full scope of humanity. Past, present or future.

If you choose to be remembered, then this is the end of the road for you. However, your life will have happened and be remembered. Your accomplishments, your friends and family will not be taken from you. Before you go, you are allowed to see all the lives you have lived, flash slowly before your eyes. Having finally chosen the mark you will leave on the earth, you cease to be, forever.

So here is the question, have you lived the life you want to be remembered for? Or would you forsake this life for another attempt?

The *Gatekeeper* grows impatient.

What do you choose...

如果你選擇轉世，那麼你前生的所有記憶和活過的痕跡就會
從地球上消失。你的孩子將會變成其他人的孩子；你的伴侶
將過著孤獨的生活，或是會愛上別人；你的成就和過失，將
會通通散落在其他人身上。你剛剛活過的一生就如從未發生
過般。你將會在人類文明以來的某個時間點上，重生成一個
新人類。也許是過去，也許是現在，或是將來。

如果你選擇被人們記住，那麼這裏就是你的終點。但是，你
的一生將會真實發生過，而且被銘記於心。你的成就、朋友
和家人都不會被帶走。在你離開之前，你的一生將會在眼前
慢慢呈現，讓你可以重溫回味。選好了留在世上的記號後，
你就永遠不再存在。

所以問題來了，你這生有過著值得被記住的生活嗎？還是你
會放棄這生，而嘗試再活一次？

看門人變得不耐煩了。

你會如何抉擇……？

The Alcoholic

"Well fuck you too!"

Martin staggered out of the office, trying to act as sober as he could, but still badly drunk from last night.

As Martin got into his car, he cried like he had never cried before. He cried as he left the car park. He cried as he swigged from his flask. And he cried all the way to the nearest bar.

He soon found himself sitting at the bar, staring mindlessly into the distance. He felt sick but he needed to keep drinking. It was the only thing that helped.

"Another?" The bartender cautiously asked.
"Yeah... keep 'em coming." Martin slurred while splashing his fifth shot against his mouth.

"You sure you're okay bud?"
"Fuck no..." A tear rolled down his cheek and into the whiskey. "My wife left me... my daughter hates me... and I just got fired!" He lifted his glass and forced a smile.

酒鬼

「去你媽媽的媽媽!」

Martin 走出辦公室,昨晚喝得爛醉的他盡可能保持清醒,但仍然有點迷糊。

Martin 上了自己的車時,就像從未哭過般嚎啕大哭。離開停車場哭了起來;拿著酒瓶大喝特喝時也哭了起來;在他向最近的酒吧前進時也一直在哭。

他很快就發現自己已經坐在酒吧裏,無意識地凝視著遠方。他有點不舒服,可是他想要繼續喝酒,因為這是唯一對他有幫助的事情。

「再來一杯?」酒保謹慎地問道。
「嗯……有多少喝多少……」Martin 邊把第五杯酒倒進嘴裏,邊含糊不清地說著。

「你真的還好嗎,老兄?」
「一點也不好……」淚珠順著他的臉頰滾進了威士忌。「妻子離開了我,女兒討厭我……而且我剛剛被解僱了!」他舉起了酒杯,強顏歡笑。

"Shit... that sucks man, here... have this next one on the house."

Martin must have passed out because the next thing he knew he was slouched in a booth, and the bartender was calling last orders.

Shambling towards the door Martin said his goodbyes and decided to finally drive home.

On the short journey home, he found himself drifting in and out of consciousness, swerving violently down the back roads to his house.

Thump Thump...

"Shit! What the fuck was that!?" Martin screamed, suddenly wide awake.

He quickly pulled over.

Wedged under his bumper was lump of bloody fur. Martin frantically searched under his car. **It was a dog. His daughter's dog.**

「真是糟透了，那一定很難過吧⋯⋯來，這一杯我們請你喝。」

Martin 肯定是昏過去了，因為接下來他知道的事，是他歪歪斜斜地坐在卡座，而酒保正在告知顧客即將打烊，問他們有沒有需要最後一次點酒。

Martin 步履蹣跚地走向門口，跟酒保說了再見，終於決定要開車回家。

在回家的短途路上，他發現自己時而昏迷，時而清醒，然後突然從偏徑上猛烈地轉向自己的房子。

隆隆——

「靠！那是甚麼鬼東西啊！？」Martin 尖叫著，瞬間清醒過來。

他迅速把車子停在路邊。

車子的保險槓下，有一團血肉蜷縮著。Martin 馬上瘋狂地查看著車子，卻發現那是一隻小狗，**他女兒的小狗**。

"You stupid mutt... how'd you get out again?" Tears welled in his eyes. "Lacy is gonna go ballistic..."

After a brief struggle with getting the dog into his trunk, Martin continued home. He had no idea what he was going to tell Lacy in the morning. A thousand excuses ran through his mind.

When he got home he went straight to the kitchen to grab more whiskey. A note was stuck to the fridge. He snatched it off and stumbled to the front room, falling into his chair.

Dear Dad,

I can't do this anymore, the drinking has gotten too much. When mom was here atleast she could help, but now...

I've gone to live with aunt Liv. I hope you get better.

Lacy

"That's just fucking great." Martin muttered before swigging from the bottle.

「你這笨蛋雜種狗⋯⋯怎麼又走出來了？」淚水湧上眼眶的他道：「Lacy 肯定會氣死我了⋯⋯」

一輪努力之後，他終於把小狗放進車尾箱，然後 Martin 便繼續駛回家。他不知道明天早上該和 Lacy 說些甚麼，腦海中浮現了一千個藉口。

他回家了以後，便直接走到廚房拿了威士忌繼續喝。冰箱門貼著一張便條。他把便條扯下來，踉蹌地走到前室，跌坐在椅子上。

親愛的爸爸，

我無法再這樣繼續下去了，酗酒的問題也越來越嚴重了。以前媽媽在這裏的時候，她至少可以幫忙，但現在⋯⋯

我搬到 Liv 阿姨那邊住了。希望你會好起來。

Lacy

「這下真是他媽的太棒了。」Martin 喃喃道，然後把威士忌大口大口地喝下去。

The rest of the night Martin drowned his sorrows with whiskey, to keep from drowning in tears.

Knock Knock...

Martin woke up on the floor. It was still night. Flashing lights crept in through the window. He stumbled to the door. It was Bill Robson, the deputy sheriff.

"Hey Martin..." Bill sighed.
"Hey... what's going on?" Martin drunkenly mumbled.

"I'm afraid... it's Lacy... she's dead."
"Wha... what happened..." Martin began to cry.

"Hit and run... we found her on the side of the road. Looks like she was walking the dog... she had a broken leash in her hand."

那晚剩下的時間，Martin 不想讓眼淚淹沒自己的悲傷，而是選擇了用威士忌。

叩叩——

Martin 在地板上醒過來，時間仍然是晚上。閃爍的燈光從窗戶透進房子。他跌跌撞撞地走到門口。站在門外的是副警長 Bill Robson。

「嘿，Martin……」Bill 嘆了口氣。
「嘿，怎麼了嗎？」Martin 醉醺醺地嘟嚷著。

「我恐怕……Lacy 她……她死了。」
「甚麼……發生甚麼事了……」Martin 哭了起來。

「肇事逃逸……我們在路邊發現她，她手裏握著一條破損的狗帶，看起來正在遛狗……」

Nobody's Perfect

I got a D-, and the teacher told me that nobody's perfect.
I lost my hat, and my mom told me that nobody's perfect.
I shattered a vase, and my grandmother told me that nobody's perfect.

I've made a lot of mistakes over my life, and I've always wished I could stop. **I've always wished that I could be perfect.**

I forgot my wallet, and my girlfriend told me that nobody's perfect.
I burnt the turkey, and the visitors told me that nobody's perfect.
I went over the speed limit, and the officer told me that nobody's perfect.

Nobody's perfect, but that doesn't mean nobody can be perfect. I will become perfect. I will get rid of all of the hopeless mistakes.

I dropped my popcorn, and the person next to me told me that nobody's perfect.
I was late to my son's soccer match, and he told me that nobody's perfect.
I broke my leg, and the doctors told me that nobody's perfect.

無人完美

我得了個 D-，老師安慰我說沒有人是完美的。
我弄丟了帽子，媽媽安慰我說沒有人是完美的。
我打破了花瓶，婆婆安慰我說沒有人是完美的。

雖然我過去的人生充滿過失，但我不想再犯錯了，**我希望自己可以當一個完美的人。**

我忘了帶銀包，女朋友安慰我說沒有人是完美的。
我把火雞烤焦了，客人安慰我說沒有人是完美的。
我超速駕駛了，警察安慰我說沒有人是完美的。

沒有人是完美的，但並不代表沒有人能達致完美。我會變成完美的人，我會擺脫所有無可救藥的錯誤。

我失手掉下了爆米花，鄰座的人安慰我說沒有人是完美的。
我錯過了兒子的足球比賽，他安慰我說沒有人是完美的。
我摔斷了腿，醫生安慰我說沒有人是完美的。

I met an old lady on the sidewalk today. I walked her home. She grinned at me suspiciously and whispered that I had 3 wishes.

I wished to be perfect.

I screamed in horror, in pain, as my skin started burning off of my body, reducing into nothing. I fell to the ground, begging for help, cursing at the old lady as my entire body began to self destruct before my eyes. Coughing up quickly dissolving blood, I collapsed, motionless, my vision starting to fade as the horrific pain started to take over.

And just like that, I disappeared without a trace.

Nobody's perfect.

今天我在路上碰到了一個老婦人，陪伴她走回家後，她帶著可疑的笑容跟我說，我可以許三個願望。

我希望成為完美的人。

我的皮膚被烈火吞噬得一點也不剩，火燒的劇痛遍布全身，我驚恐得不停尖叫。我倒了在地上，乞求上天放過我。在咒罵著那個老婦人的同時，我眼巴巴地看著自己整個身軀在自毀：急速溶解的血液令我不停咳嗽、意識開始離我而去、身體再也動不了、視野開始消退……只剩下殘酷的煎熬蓋過一切感官。

就是這樣，我消失得無影無蹤。

沒有人是完美的。

I Have Seven Minutes Before I Die

You know, I always wondered how I would go.

I decided, as much as it was possible to decide, that I wanted to die on my own terms, not suffering in a hospital bed. Once life began to become unbearable, I'd finish myself off in my car. I heard it was peaceful and completely painless. You simply... slip away.

No, I know what you're expecting. This isn't an account of the hell after suicide, nor of a life trapped in limbo. If it was... well, you'd never know, anyway.

It happened quickly. I was 25. Am, 25. I doubt I'll ever see 26.

Do you know how much courage a person needs to kill themselves?

The body rebels. The flesh understands the instructions sent by the brain, but not the reasons behind them; after all, their control mechanism is the very thing taking away their control. There is a kind of morbid poetry to that, one that I am not comfortable exploring.

It took me almost an hour to fit the pipe onto the exhaust. In that time, someone walked by, looking into my garage for

死前七分鐘

你知道嗎？我總是在想我會是怎麼死的。

我決定好了，我希望盡可能地按照自己的意願死去，而不是在病床上受盡折磨。一旦生活開始變得難以承受，我就會在車子裏了結自己的生命。我聽說那樣會很平靜，而且完全無痛，性命只會悄然流逝掉。

不是的，我知道你在期待些甚麼。可是我不是要描述自殺後的地獄，也不是要訴説被困監獄的生活。如果是的話⋯⋯呃，我也就無法在這裏跟你分享了吧。

事情來得很急。我現在二十五歲。不知道還能不能活到二十六歲。

你知道一個人需要鼓起多大的勇氣才能自殺嗎？

身體會自我排斥。肌肉理解大腦發出的指示，但不理解背後的原因。畢竟，控制肌肉的機制正正是在剝奪肌肉的控制權。我知道有一種專門寫這類題材的病態詩歌，可是我不太想去研究它們。

我花了將近一個小時，才把管子安裝到車子的排氣管上。我在忙著裝管子的時候，有人走了過來，瞥看了我的車庫一眼。

the slightest instant. We locked eyes, and I think I caught a glimpse of realization in his look. Then again, maybe it was something else. I've never been good with people. He hurried away, though. Even now, I wonder if he'll ever regret his decision to not interfere.

I doubt he'll ever care.

With a car of my size and the tight emission rules for vehicles, carbon monoxide poisoning will set in within 15 minutes.

Irreversible brain damage occurs before that limit is up.

You know what's the worst thing?

I've read about how suicide survivors often realize that **all their problems in life can be solved through simply staying alive.** Death by carbon monoxide poisoning was brutal in the sense that one had to willfully sit in the car over some time before he could die.

That sense of realization only hit me 8 minutes into my suicide attempt.

Now.

我們四目交投，他的表情好像告訴我，他知道了我要幹甚麼。
不過也許是我的誤解罷了，我從來不擅於與人相處。他也匆
匆離開了。即使是現在，我也在想，不知道他會否後悔自己
決定不干涉我的行為呢？

雖然我不覺得他會為我煩心。

以我這部車子的尺寸和它嚴格的排放規格來算，十五分鐘內
我就會因吸入過量一氧化碳中毒身亡。

這段時間內將會造成無法復原的腦創傷。

你知道最糟糕的是甚麼嗎？

我讀過一些自殺倖存者的言論，他們自殺不遂後大多都會意
識到，**原來只要還活著，生活中的所有問題都會迎刃而解**。
利用一氧化碳中毒自殺是很殘酷的做法，因為自殺者必須執
意地坐在車廂裏一段時間才會死去。

在我自殺途中，只花了八分鐘，我就意識到那些自殺倖存者
的領悟了。

那麼。

How long does it take before permanent brain damage occurs?

I can't seem to remember. Should I get out now? I don't really want to take that chance. Life was hard enough before.

But dear god, am I terrified of death.

要多長時間才會造成永久性腦創傷啊？

我好像無法回想起來呢。我應該現在出去嗎？我真的不想冒這個險啊，生活已經夠艱難了。

可是，親愛的上帝啊，我真害怕死亡啊。

Just 60 Seconds

"Hey, erm, Dave? Could you help me..."
"Not right now, Jane. There's something going on. Look, it's all over the news..."

I couldn't take my eyes off the screen. I didn't even turn around, just grabbed the remote and turned up the volume so she could hear too.

"...Dr. Jenner, if we follow your guidelines, what are the probabilities of survival do you think?"

"I honestly can't say this as absolute fact because we know hardly anything about this, hence why we're calling them, guidelines. But, from the tests we've been able to perform so far, I do believe that if you follow all of them, you'll have a much higher chance of survival. What we are certain of, is it will be gone within the next 20 to 24 hours."

"Can we have a copy of the guidelines on screen, please?...There we go, thank-you... Dr. Jenner, would you mind going over all these points for the people at home?"

"Certainly. Okay, number one, the most important; DO NOT go outside. Plain and simple, just, don't, do it!...Number two; DO NOT drink any water that has come from the tap. Boiling the water won't help either. It is important to keep together! So stay with your family and friends, call others on the phone and spread the word. Number three;..."

只得六十秒

「嘿，呃，Dave？你能幫我一下……」

「現在不行啊，Jane。有些事情發生了。看吧，新聞都在鋪天蓋地報道著……」

我無法把目光從屏幕上移開。我甚至沒有轉身，只是伸手拿了遙控器並將音量調高，讓她也可以聽得到廣播。

「……Jenner博士，如果跟從你所提出的指引，你認為生存的概率有多少？」

「老實說，我不能說這是絕對的事實，因為我們幾乎對此一無所知，所以我們只能稱它們為指引。但是，從迄今為止我們能做的測試來看，我相信如果跟從所有要點，便會提高生存的機會。我們確定的是，它會在未來二十到二十四小時內消失。」

「可以把指南的副本放到在屏幕上嗎？……有了，謝謝你……Jenner博士，你可以為家裏的觀眾們複習一次所有要點嗎？」

「當然可以。好吧，第一點，也是最重要的一點：不要外出。簡單又容易，只是不・要・外・出！……第二點：不要喝水龍頭的自來水。即使把水煮沸也無濟於事。團結在一起也是非常重要的！所以請與家人和朋友待在一起，打電話給其他人並廣傳這個訊息。第三點：……」

"Dave,"
"Shh!"

"...and windows. Wrap towels or thick sheets in plastic bags, and stuff them into every crack. You need to make your home as air tight as possible. If anyone thinks of a better solution, please, don't hesitate to call in and share."

"Go and get all the towels and blankets from the cupboard...and plastic bags!" I still couldn't take my eyes off the screen.

"...rash is instantaneous. Next, they'll become paralyzed from the neck down as the toxins take over the nervous system. If the person has reached this symptom, I'm afraid it's too late. They'll fall limp, with fast and raspy breathing, followed by cardiac arrest."

The doctor looked away from the camera for a few seconds before continuing.

"You will have just 60 seconds from this point to remove yourselves from the corpse, otherwise..."

「Dave⋯⋯」
「噓！！！」

「⋯⋯和窗戶。用塑料袋把毛巾或厚床單包裹起來，然後將它們塞進每一個裂縫裏。請你務必盡可能地讓房子弄得密不透風。如果有人想到更好的解決方案，請不要猶豫，請立即打電話過來跟我們分享。」

「去拿櫥櫃裡的所有毛巾和毯子⋯⋯還有塑料袋！」我仍然死盯著屏幕，目光無法移開。

「⋯⋯會即時出現皮疹。接下來，當毒素接管神經系統時，患者們頸部以下就會癱瘓。如果患者已經出現這種症狀，我恐怕為時已晚。他們接著會瘸著腳走，發出急促且刺耳的呼吸聲，最後是心臟驟停。」

醫生頓了一頓，他有幾秒鐘沒有看鏡頭，然後才繼續說下去。

「從那一刻起，你只有六十秒時間，請在限時內儘快遠離那具屍體，否則⋯⋯」

"DAVE!!!"

"Jesus Christ! WHAT?!" I finally turned around. My wife had the rash all over her face and fell to the floor as soon as I turned.

The rash had instantly opened into sores on her body and oozed white, foamy pus. The layers of skin began to melt and her eyes rolled back into her head. Her body would not stop shaking.

I ran...

I ran into the kitchen like some petrified dog. I ran into the kitchen to save myself.

The 60 second mark was approaching, I never heard what Dr. Jenner said, but I knew it wouldn't be anything good.

My eyes quickly panned the room. I saw the back door, (Do not go outside!), I saw the empty, just used glass next to the sink, (do not drink the water!) And then I saw my wife again...

「DAVE！！！」

「老天爺啊！怎麼回事？！」我終於轉過身來。我的妻子臉上全是皮疹，我一轉身她便倒在地上。

她身上的皮疹馬上變成了開放性的傷口，更滲出白色泡沫狀的膿液。她的皮膚開始融化，眼睛也反白了，身體不斷顫抖著。

我拔足狂奔⋯⋯

我像一隻被嚇壞了的狗般跑進了廚房；我為了自保所以跑進了廚房。

快要到六十秒的界限了，雖然我聽不到 Jenner 博士說之後會怎樣，但我知道那不會是甚麼好東西。

我的雙眼快速地張望著房間。我看到了後門（不要外出！），看到水槽旁邊有個剛剛用完的玻璃杯（不要喝自來水！）。然後又看到了妻子⋯⋯

Value Humanity
别 低 估 人 性

I Got a Sound Wave Tattoo, But the Audio Came Out Wrong

My senior year of college, my mom died suddenly. So, a few months after the burial, I decided to get a tattoo to remember her.

I thought about getting her favorite flowers, her astrological sign, her signature….then I read about sound wave tattoos online. They sounded perfect. I could get a recording of her voice tattooed on me, forever. For the first time since she died, I felt like I might be able to start healing.

I found a shop nearby that was certified to give sound wave tattoos and met with my artist. The tattoo itself only took twenty minutes, but it was my first tattoo, so twenty minutes was enough.

After a few days, once the tattoo was 'activated' by the app designers, I played it for the first time. **Tears burned at the corners of my eyes when her voice streamed out of my phone, clear and confident.**

"Hi honey! I love you! I hope you have a great day!"

I'd play the audio a couple of times a week, not wanting to get bored with it. When my dad came to visit me a few weeks later, I made sure to show him.

聲軌紋身

臨近我大學畢業的那年，媽媽突然去世了。在葬禮的幾個月後，我決定弄一個紋身來紀念她。

至於紋身的圖案，我想過用她最喜歡的花、她的星座或是她的簽名。可當我在網上看到有關聲軌紋身的資訊，我覺得太棒了！我想用她的錄音弄一個永久紋身。自從她去世以來，這是我第一次感覺到自己開始好過來了。

我在附近找到了一家有「聲軌紋身認證」的店，會見了我的紋身師。紋身只用了二十分鐘就弄好了，可這是我第一次紋身，二十分鐘就像二十小時那麼久。

幾天後，程式設計員把紋身「激活」了，作為第一個使用者的我就播放它。**當我聽見她的聲音從我電話傳出時，我的淚水不禁奪眶而出。**

她的聲音既清晰又有自信：「嗨親愛的，我愛你！祝你今天過得開心！」

因為很怕會厭倦了媽媽的聲音，所以我一個星期只會把音頻播放幾次就夠了。幾週後，爸爸來探望我，我說好了會給他聽聽看。

"Hi honey! I love you! I hope – **KRRKKKK!!!**"

Surprised at the sudden static, I raised my eyes to meet his. We shared a dismayed look. When the audio continued to play, I jumped. It was still my mother's voice, but she was screaming and crying.

"*I don't know what I did to either one of you,*" she sobbed. "*You won't get away with this. I'll get someone to look under the sycamore. You won't get away with this.*"

Eyes still locked, mine widened at the mention of the sycamore.

"*I'm your family. I'm your only family,*" she continued; her voice shuddered with grief. "*How could you do this to me? You won't get away with this. You won't get away with this….*"

Then, silence.

After a few moments, my father stood up. "We'll have to move the body soon, you know. Saturday good for you?"

「嗨親愛的，我愛你！祝你──咔咔咔咔！！！」

我被突然的停頓嚇倒了，我抬起頭看著爸爸，我們一臉鬱悶的對望著。當音頻繼續播放下去時，我嚇得心跳也漏了一拍。播放著的，仍是媽媽的聲音，可是卻變成了她的尖叫聲和哭泣聲。

「*我得罪你們了嗎？*」她低泣著說：「*你們逃不掉的，我會找人來看看梧桐樹的底下。你們逃不掉的。*」

我和爸爸還是對望著，可是我聽見「梧桐樹」的時候眼睛不禁睜大了。

「*我是你們的家人，唯一的家人。*」她的聲音悲傷得顫抖起來，續說：「*你們怎可以這樣對我？你們逃不掉的，你們逃不掉的……*」

接下來是一片寂靜。

過了一會兒，爸爸站了起來。「我們要盡快把屍體移走。星期六你有空嗎？」

There's a Child Abuser in My Home

On a typical day, there are more than 20,000 phone calls placed to domestic violence hotlines nationwide.

I'd probably account for one or two of them-- if I were stupid enough to call for help.

In domestic violence homicides, women are six times more likely to be killed when there is a gun in the house.

If I could, I'd get rid of it. **Someone like him shouldn't have access to a gun in the first place**, but I figure that's just my bad luck.

Domestic victimization is correlated with a higher rate of depression and suicidal behavior.

Ain't that the truth. You know it gets really bad when you're more scared of being alive than whatever pains death may bring.

He wasn't like this at first. He was a thin-framed kinda thing. Cuter, too. **I guess the increase in bulk bolstered his boldness. Youth correlates with foolishness and irrationality,** I suppose, but his decisions are rather violent. Drop a dish, get punched in the face. Get home from work too late, get punched in the face. More serious "infractions" result in him

兒童虐待案

一般情況下，全國有關家庭暴力的熱線，每天都會接到超過二萬個電話報案。

如果我笨得致電求助的話，我可能也會是其中一兩個報案紀錄吧。

在家庭暴力兇殺案中，要是屋子裏有槍的話，女性被殺的可能性是屋子裏沒有槍的六倍。

如果可以的話，我也想逃離家庭暴力的魔掌。首先，**像他這種人根本不應該有使用槍械的權利**，不過後來我意識到只是我不幸。

家庭暴力與抑鬱和自殺行為有密切關係，前者會導致後兩者的發生率較高。

難道不對嗎？你試想想，當一個人害怕活著，多於害怕死亡帶來的痛苦時，是有多麼的難過吧。

起初他不是這樣的。他本來瘦瘦弱弱，也比較可愛。隨著他的塊頭越來越大，他的膽子好像也隨之變大了。**也許青春總是離不開愚蠢和非理性吧，但他的決定卻相當暴力。**掉了盤子，臉就被揍一拳。下班回家太晚了，臉也被揍一拳。如果

threatening us with the gun.

Unfortunately, Henry and I are pretty accustomed to this.

He's a lot rougher with Henry than he is with me, like, on purpose. **He feels like he has to assert his dominance and affirm with Henry that he's undeniably the man of the house.**

I've tried to help him, of course, but usually that resulted in a black eye. I'm at a loss, and Henry's self-confidence has nosedived. Friends have advised us in the past-- "intervention", "call the police", "stay with us for a bit"-- but they couldn't possibly understand our position.

They don't realize how incredibly demonic this person is, and how determined he is to keep us firmly under his thumb.

Sometimes Henry will cry out of nowhere because of how terrified he is. I try to soothe him, remind him that men shouldn't cry, that he needs to be brave. He gets angry if he hears Henry cry. Then comes the verbal abuse.

Maybe a kick in the stomach or two to keep him quiet for the rest of the night. When I take Henry back to our room, I soothe him the best I can. The years of torment have pretty

我們不小心做了其他更嚴重的「違規行為」，他便會用槍威脅我們。

不幸的是，我和 Henry 對這件事已經有點習以為常。

他和 Henry 單獨相處的時候，會比和我一起時更加粗暴，他好像是故意這樣對 Henry 的。**他覺得必須確立自己的主導權，並向 Henry 宣稱自己才是一家之主。**

我當然曾經試圖幫助他，但通常會換來瘀青發黑的眼圈。我感到很茫然，Henry 的自信心也一落千丈。過去的日子裏，朋友們曾建議我們「介入治療」、「報警」、「過來與我們待一會兒」等等，但他們始終無法理解我們的立場。

他們意識不到這個人其實邪惡得令人難以置信，也不知道他有多希望我們可以一直受他擺布。

有時候，Henry 會突然因心中的恐懼而哭泣。我試圖安慰他，提醒他作為男子漢不應該哭，應該勇敢面對。要是他聽見 Henry 的哭聲，他便會暴怒起來，然後辱罵他。

也許還會往 Henry 的肚子踢個一兩下，讓 Henry 在餘下的夜裏都保持安靜。當我把 Henry 帶回到我們的房間時，我

much broken him, though. There's only so much more he can take, and I'm reaching my limits as well, both physically and mentally.

As much as we'd like to escape this hell, our options are narrow, if not nonexistent. But what can we do?

He's only twelve, and his father and I have no idea how he got like this.

竭盡所能地安慰他。可是，長年累月的折磨快要擊潰他了，他不能再承受更多了，而且我也身心俱疲，快要達到極限了。

儘管我們有多想擺脫這個地獄，但我們只得有限的選擇，能想出來的都已想過了。我們還能做些甚麼呢？

他只有十二歲而已，我跟他爸都不知道為何他會變成這樣。

Smith & Wesson

Right 23, left 48, right 32.

Michael Bartlett was a good man. A good father. He worked at a deli that his family had built from the ground up. He spent his weekends playing golf and going to the gun range with his friends.

Right 34, left 19, right 21.

Although he had his work, and his hobbies, nothing came before his daughter. She was his entire world since the day she was born, and reminded him of her mother every day.

Right 45, left 31, right 33.

He had longed for his wife ever since her passing. She was one of the first to succumb to the virus. He was always thankful that she wasn't around to see the cities fall. To see what the virus made humans capable of doing to their fellow man.

Right 17, left 26, right 43.

He and his daughter had been hiding in their home for a few weeks before the infected developed an interest in the old place. And having shot every last bullet in the house, they

槍櫃

右二十三，左四十八，右三十二。

Michael Bartlett 是個好好先生兼慈父，他在家人白手興家的熟食店裏工作，週末跟朋友打打高爾夫球、到靶場練練槍。

右三十四，左十九，右二十一。

雖然他有自己的工作，也熱衷於自己的嗜好，但一切都不及自己的女兒重要。自從女兒出生那天起，她便成為了 Michael 的全世界，而且每天也令 Michael 想起妻子。

右四十五，左三十一，右三十三。

妻子過世後，Michael 一直對她念念不忘。妻子是首批病患者之一，他很慶幸妻子不用目睹城市墮落的那些時刻，也不用見證人類因病毒肆虐，導致失去常性，殘忍對待自己同伴的慘況。

右十七，左二十六，右四十三。

在疫情蔓延前幾個星期，Michael 跟女兒早已躲了在家。眼看屋子裏的子彈都用光了，他們陷入窘境。Michael 被咬傷了，可是他很驚訝被咬後的感覺跟他想像的不一樣。沒有劇

were quickly overwhelmed. Michael had been bitten, and was surprised at how it felt. Not a sharp pain, no searing burn, but more of a dull, freezing, sensation. As if he had submerged his ankle into a bathtub filled with ice water.

Right 44, left 11, right 13.

Before the bite overcame him completely, he had told his daughter he loved her and wanted the best for her no matter what. He prayed she believed him as he locked her in his gun safe and sent out a distress signal over the radio with his last breaths of sanity.

He yearned for death, anything to keep him from becoming like the monsters that surrounded him, but death never came. His mind finally left him, but not before hearing his daughter's muffled scream from inside the gun safe one last time. He used to soothe her fears, and now he was the root of them.

Right 13, left 6, right 33.

Click.

痛，也感覺不到灼熱，只有種像泡在冰水般，深入骨髓的冰冷感。

右四十四，左十一，右十三。

趁病毒還未完全佔據自己之前，Michael 跟女兒表示自己很愛她，而且無論如何也想把最好的都給她。他把女兒鎖進槍櫃，然後用僅餘的理智通過收音機發出求救信號，當時他向上天禱告女兒會相信自己的決定。

他一心求死，想從即將成為怪物的恐懼中得到解脫，可是死神沒有找上他。意識消退之前，Michael 聽到女兒的尖叫聲從槍櫃裏傳出。以前他會安撫女兒，替她驅趕恐懼，現在的他卻成為了恐懼本身。

右十三，左六，右三十三。

嗒。

I Witnessed Everything Over Skype

I am a young man in my mid-twenties, the typical kind. I had a girlfriend, until she was killed in her own room, thousands of miles from me. But I witnessed everything over Skype.

It was a late autumn afternoon. I sat down on the couch with my laptop, pressed Call on Skype. Me and my girl, we had been in this relationship for longer than most people would expect from a pair of millennials living in the opposite sides of the globe.

This Skype thing, for us, was a kind of scheduled daily ritual that bridged the distance and sustained the love. A healthy habit.

The ringing tone stretched out into what sounded like millennia. I smiled, getting ready to greet her blissful face, always too close to the camera. That was what special about her, a certain clumsiness and innocence oozing out from every little things she did. From the big brown sparkly eyes. From the unkempt baby hairs. **From the killer smile, that...**

My thoughts was violently interrupted when a masked figure appeared on the call window. I yelped, but the deep dark stare from behind the eye cutouts stayed undisturbed.

我在 Skype 目睹了一切

我是一個二十多歲、很典型的那種年輕人。我本來有個女朋友，直到她與我隔著數千英里之遙時，在自己的房間被殺。而我就在 Skype 目睹了一切。

那天是一個深秋的下午，我坐在沙發上用著筆記本電腦，然後在 Skype 上按下「撥打」。我跟女朋友也是千禧世代，而且相隔半個地球，大部分人也認為我們不會長久吧，可是我們在一起已經很久了。

對我們來說，用 Skype 對話已是每天必做的事了，這樣做不但能把我們遠距離的心靈連結起來，還能讓我們好好維繫彼此的愛。這算是個健康的習慣吧。

來電鈴聲聽起來很懷舊，讓我想了千禧年代的回憶。我微笑著，準備迎接她那總是太近鏡頭，卻滿是幸福的臉蛋。這正是她的特別之處，她所做的每一件小事，都流露著一種笨拙又天真無邪的氣質。就像她那雙閃閃發光的棕色大眼睛；就像她髮際那些蓬亂的碎髮；**就像殺手的微笑，那……**

我腦海裏一切的想法，都被眼前這個出現在通話視窗的面具人統統嚇跑了。我驚呼了一下，但這雙面具下的眼睛卻無動於衷，只繼續陰沉地凝視著我。

It looked unapologetically at the camera, then slowly backed up, letting the whole scene to be captured. My heart tensed.

My girlfriend was lying on her bed, motionless. The masked thing grabbed and jerked her head up to look directly at me.

Its finger pointed at the bloody mess that was once her throat, then moved up to its lips in a shushing gesture. The brutality of the scene paralysed me in my seat.

I covered my mouth with my hands to stop myself from vomiting. My eyes stayed fixed and frozen on the surreal sight in front of me. A silent scream was lost amid a vortex of emotions inside my brain.

The masked killer dropped my girlfriend's head, winked at me, then quietly backed out of the room.

Silence.

I was left there staring at the corpse of the girl I loved, lying on a bed that turned crimson from her blood. A physical metaphor for the bed of roses I once promised her.

這雙毫無歉意的眼睛直直地看著鏡頭，然後慢慢退後，讓整個場景都能清晰地拍下來。看得我心臟都緊繃了。

女朋友躺在床上，一動不動。面具人抓住了她的頭，猛地拉起，讓她抬起頭直視著我。

他用手指指向她的喉嚨位置，現在只見一片鮮血淋漓，然後把手指放回自己的嘴唇位置，擺出噓聲的姿勢。殘暴又血腥的畫面使我癱坐在椅上。

我用雙手搗住嘴巴，不讓自己吐出來。目睹眼前這一切感覺很不真實的東西，我的目光停住了。內心翻起了一股情緒漩渦，吞沒了我腦海裏那無聲的尖叫。

面具殺手鬆開了手，讓女朋友的頭掉回床上，然後向我眨了眨眼，再悄悄地走出了房間。

一片死寂。

面具人撇下了我，由得我眼巴巴地盯著那具屬於我所愛的女孩的屍體，躺在因染血而變成深紅色的床上。我曾經答應過她，會用鋪滿玫瑰的床來給她驚喜，現在竟然這樣應驗了。

"You got what you deserve, you unfaithful bitch!" I thought bitterly and pressed End Call. I sipped my coffee, satisfied, not letting my guilt to take over the pleasure.

I gave myself a 10/10 for such a genius plan of hiring an assassin to murder my cheating girlfriend. All I needed to do now was to pick up the phone and called her local police station, and to play the role of a distraught witness, thousands of miles away.

The phone rang as I was reaching for it. Mildly perplexed, I took the call.

"Hey, it's me. It looks like someone is with her. A man. Probably her new, you know, guy. We have to postpone the surprise party today. Speak later", the distorted voice of the assassin I hired whispered down the line.

「這是你應得的報應，你這不忠的臭婊子！」我心裏氣憤地想著，按下了「結束通話」。感到很滿意的我，呷了一口咖啡，不讓內疚感蓋過快感。

僱用殺手來殺掉出軌的女友——這個天才計劃，我給自己滿分！現在我要做的，只是拿起電話，撥號到她當地的警察局報案，扮演一個在千里之外、極其不安的目擊證人。

當我伸手去拿電話時，它就響了。我有點茫然，但還是接過了電話。

*「嗨，是我。看來有人和她在一起，是個男人，應該是，呃，新獵物吧。今天這個驚喜派對要推遲了，待會再聊吧。」*話筒傳來的，是受僱於我那位殺手的失真聲線。

I Believe in You

"..."

"Ah I see, it didn't go well again, did it?"

"..."

"Hey hey don't cry, it's okay. So what if you messed up again? Failure is just the first step to success. Keep trying and I know you'll succeed."

"..."

"Hey. Don't let anyone tell you what you can or can't do! Remember that okay? I believe in you. So definitely believe in yourself. You can do this."

"..."

"Alice you know I'm always there for you, you don't need to thank me. Call me again if you need help or support, okay?"

It would have been a week later after that call, **tears started welling up in my eyes as I read the headline of the daily news.**

堅定的信心

「……」

「噢，我知道了，你又遇到瓶頸了吧？」

「……」

「嘿，別哭別哭，沒事的。就算你再搞砸了，也沒甚麼大不了吧？失敗乃成功之母啊，只要有恆心，你一定可以順利完成的！」

「……」

「嘿，別讓其他人指揮你的人生，要記住這點啊，知道嗎？我對你有信心的，所以你也要對自己有信心，你可以辦到的！」

「……」

「我會一直支持你的，Alice。不用感謝我了，如果你需要任何幫助或支援的話，你再打給我吧！」

接過那通電話後一個星期，**我看到每日新聞的標題，淚水開始湧到眼眶。**

"Woman Found Dead in her Apartment"
"24 year old Alice Donnel was found collapsed at kitchen counter...."
"...complaints of rotting odor coming from the apartment..."
"...cause of the death is suspected to be overdose..."

It was hard holding back the tears. I couldn't have been more proud of her than this moment.

I knew she could do it.

「*女子倒斃寓所　列屍體發現案*」
「*24 歲女子 Alice Donnel 被發現倒斃於廚房櫃台旁⋯⋯*」
「*⋯⋯附近居民投訴該寓所傳出腐爛異味⋯⋯*」
「*⋯⋯死因暫時列作過量服藥⋯⋯*」

我強忍著不哭，但還是禁不住流淚了，此刻的我實在太以她為榮了。

我早就知道她能做到的。

The Red Water Lily

At age 12 I found a red water lily floating in the canal close to my house. The colours were rich and vibrant, the deepest shade of vermilion I'd ever come across in nature. It was so vivid that it seemed unnaturally so, like someone had manufactured it in a lab and then placed it there for all the enjoy.

I passed that red water lily every day of the summer holidays. As the days wore on, so did my fascination with it. I found myself drawn to it, unable to take my eyes off it.

Under my gaze **the flower seemed to pulse with life, its petals deepening so that they appeared black** until I blinked and suddenly they were red again. It was the only red lily in the entire canal. Unique. Special. Mine.

I spent my nights studying horticulture. Nowhere could I find anything about the red water lily, but I learnt all I could about the environments they grew in, what seasons they bloomed in, even how to grow my own. Our backyard had a tiny pond. If I could somehow steal the lily and transplant it into my own yard, it could be mine and mine alone. Forever.

Two weeks before summer ended I took the plunge, literally. I followed the lily's roots down, careful not to disturb them for fear I might harm the plant.

紅睡蓮

十二歲那年，我在靠近家的運河上，發現了一朵紅色的睡蓮
在河面漂浮著。紅睡蓮的顏色既濃郁又鮮艷，是我在大自然
裏看到過最深的朱紅色。它耀眼得有點不自然，像是有人在
實驗室製造了這朵睡蓮後，把它放在河裏供人欣賞似的。

暑假的每一天，我都會經過運河，看見那朵紅睡蓮。隨著歲
月的流逝，我對它日久生情了。我發現自己被睡蓮迷倒了，
視線無法離開它。

在我眼裏，**紅睡蓮看似充滿生命力般，花瓣顏色逐漸加深，
深得看起來似是黑色的。**可是當我一眨眼，花瓣又會突然變
回紅色。它是整條運河中唯一一朵紅睡蓮。獨一無二、與別
不同、屬於我的。

我花了無數個夜晚學習園藝。我找不到任何關於紅睡蓮的資
料，可是我盡所能學會了有關睡蓮的生長環境、開花期，更
學會了如何自行種植。我們的後院有一個小池塘，如果我能
把紅睡蓮偷回來，並將它移植到我家的池塘的話，它就是屬
於我的了，而且只會屬於我一人，直到永遠。

在夏天結束前兩週，我縱身跳入河裏。我沿著睡蓮的根莖游
下去，小心翼翼地不想觸碰到它，生怕會傷害到它。

I knew they would be embedded in the canal floor, and if I could uproot them gently, the flower would be mine.

The canal was deeper than I expected, and as my hands touched the bottom, I realised the roots weren't buried there, but in the side. No big deal. I wrapped my hand around them, braced against the wall, and pulled.

Nothing.

I yanked harder. The roots were embedded deep. I scratched at the dirt, but rather than dislodging it, my fingers went through it. It wasn't dirt. It was a hemp. A sack, to be exact, lodged in the canal wall. I let go of the roots and tore it open.

I screamed, water filling my nose and mouth and lungs. A gaunt white face stared back at me. **The lily's roots were buried deep in its neck.**

The murder was never solved, and I never got my flower. I couldn't stop thinking about it though. I dreamt about it, night after night, for years. It consumed me.

The flower died once the body was removed, and its beauty with it.

我知道睡蓮的根莖會嵌到運河的地板上，要是我能溫柔地把它們連根拔起，這朵花就會屬於我的了。

運河比我想像的還要深，當我用手碰到運河底部時，我才發現睡蓮的根莖不是埋在那裏，而是在旁邊。沒甚麼大問題嘛。於是我用雙手包圍著根莖，以牆作支撐，然後用力拉。

甚麼也沒有。

我更用力地猛拉著，看來根莖嵌得非常深。我沒有移動它，只撬了撬旁邊的泥土，但我的手指穿過了它。那不是泥土，而是一些麻類植物。準確地說，是一個卡在運河牆壁上的麻袋子。我鬆開了抓著根莖的手，然後撕開了麻袋子。

我尖叫著，河水馬上湧進了我的鼻子、嘴巴和肺部。只見一張憔悴的白臉凝視著我。**睡蓮的根莖，深深埋在他的脖子裏。**

謀殺案破解不了，我也得不到我的花。可是我還是不自控地想起那朵紅睡蓮。這麼多年來，我夜復一夜地夢見它。它吞噬了我。

一旦那具屍體被移除，花就會枯萎，它的美態也會隨之而消失。

I've spent my life trying to figure out how the flower got its unique colour. How the roots embedded themselves in the body, how they drew nutrients from it. I haven't yet replicated the process, but I'll keep trying.

I discovered one vital piece of information from the police reports that I didn't know as a child. The missing piece that's kept me from my goal.

The body wasn't dead when they were buried in the canal wall.

One more try. Nobody will notice she's gone.

我耗盡一生，一直在努力研究那朵花是如何長出這般獨特的顏色，根莖又是如何嵌入人體，如何從中吸取營養。我還沒有得出結果，但我會繼續努力。

我從警方的報告中，**發**現了一道關鍵的情報，那是我小時候不知道的事。就像找到長久以來缺失了的一塊拼圖，現在完滿了。

那具屍體被埋在運河牆壁時，他還未死去的。

再試一次吧。沒有人會發現她失蹤了的。

Monsters Beneath the Surface

If you find a fisherman who isn't afraid of the ocean above all else, he's lying. Either about his fears, or about his profession.

Men who chose the sea life will often spend months without seeing dry land. During such time, there is no shortage of reminders about the respect the ocean demands.

Sometimes, when trying to sleep, you can kind of hear something swimming out there. Very near, even touching the boat, scratching the wood. **It reminds you there are monsters under the surface, that they are closer than you can imagine.**

But they could be closer still.

It was a dreary december night when a young boy called Abraham Myers joined our small crew. Strange lad, very self-absorbed, "introvert" is how you'd call it.

Queer, if you ask me, but he performed the daily jobs just fine. There was something off about him though, I knew it from the start. His eyes... they were the blackest eyes I'd ever seen. The men never sought his company much, and he never seemed to wish for it. That kid gave me the chills, I'm ashamed to admit.

藏在底下的怪物

如果你聽見一個漁民跟你説他不怕海洋的話，他肯定是在撒謊。他要麼是假裝不害怕，要麼便是假裝自己是個漁民。

選擇在海上生活的人，通常有好幾個月都不會看到乾旱的土地。航海期間，總會有些事物時刻提醒著你「欺山莫欺水」，謹記要尊重海洋。

有時當你想睡覺，你便會聽到有些東西游過的聲音。它們游得非常接近，甚至會觸摸船身，割割著船身的木材。它提醒著你，**水面之下藏著怪物，而且它們比你想像中更接近**。

它們可能近在咫尺。

十二月一個沉悶的夜晚，一個名叫 Abraham Myers 的年輕人，加入了我們人數不多的船員隊伍。他是個奇怪的小伙子，非常自我中心，別人看來會覺得是「內向」吧。

如果你問我怎麼看他，我覺得他是個同性戀者，但他平日的工作表現也不賴。不過我一開始就覺得他有點可疑，他的雙眼……是我見過的最黑的一雙眼睛。同事們只顧自己的群聚，很少找他參與，可是他似乎毫不介意。雖然很難説出口，但我必須承認：那小子讓我感到不安。

But my concerns were short lived.

In the middle of the following year we faced the kind of storm that every seafarer dreads. It arrived suddenly, mighty, and destroyed us. Everything we owned went down with that ship and our mundane worries went down along.

Only a single lifeboat escaped, holding five men among which were both me and Abraham Myers. We had no way to signal our position and get help. Something changed inside Abraham that day, he became scared, useless, paranoid. He'd cry during the night and keep us awake, he'd not help in our attempts to fish, he'd criticize all our decisions.

Ten days went by like this, ten days of little water and almost no food. **Ten days, until my breaking point.**

The others looked in disbelief when I first punched the kid down. He was crying, begging for his life and calling his mother's name. I still hear it in my dreams every night. There was not a moment of hesitation. The rest of the men soon joined in. All of them. Abraham took the beating for almost two whole minutes before finally shutting up.

但這個困惑很快就消失了。

在接下來的一年中,我們遇到了讓每個海員都聞風喪膽的風暴。它突如其來地吹襲我們,把我們徹底摧毀了。我們擁有的一切,連同心裏那些無濟於事的憂慮,都隨著那艘船沉進海底。

只有一艘救生艇成功逃脫,艇上載了五個人,當中包括我和 Abraham Myers。我們無法發出信號向他人表示我們的位置,以致求救無門。自那天開始,Abraham 的內心起了一些變化,他變得害怕、無能又偏執。他會在夜裏哭泣,吵得我們睡不著;他不會幫忙捕魚;但他對我們所有的決定都諸多批評。

他就以這副模樣過了十天,這十天只有少得可憐的水,食物也幾乎吃光了。**整整十天,我忍無可忍了。**

我再按捺不住,把那個小伙子打倒在地,當時其他人都露出難以置信的表情。他哭了起來,向我求饒,又叫著媽媽的名字。我現在每天晚上都會在夢中聽見他的哭喊聲。其他人沒有片刻猶豫,瞬間便加入戰團,全部人也加入了。在他閉嘴之前,Abraham 捱打了將近兩分鐘。

I was hungry and ripped out pieces of meat from his thighs with my teeth. So did everyone else. When I got back up, there was only a red mass where once a man's soul had lived. I stared at the others, blood on their hands, beards and faces, a trail of tears slowly making way through red cheeks. Rescue would arrive the following day.

There are monsters dwelling beneath the surface. **But they shouldn't scare you half as much as the monsters dwelling within yourself.**

我餓了，然後張口咬他的大腿，一下一下地把肉塊撕下來。其他人也照樣做。當我站起身的時候，本來那具附有靈魂的軀殼，現在變成了一團紅色的東西。我盯著其他人，他們的手、鬍鬚和臉滿是鮮血，淚水慢慢流過紅色的臉頰。救援將在翌日到達。

有些怪物住在水面之下，**可是他們的驚嚇程度，遠遠不及那些住在你心底裏的怪物。**

Everything to Lose

It was almost too good to be true. I had been having financial troubles, and then one day something appeared in the mail that would fix everything.

CONGRATULATIONS! You have been selected to appear on the game show "Everything to Lose." Huge cash prizes are awarded to the winners! Please report on May 31st, 2019 to...

And then it provided an address. I was understandably skeptical, but I was a medical student drowning in debt and really needed the money.

I arrived at the location to find a huge warehouse in an almost abandoned part of town. I wandered around inside until I discovered cameras facing a very basic set. A thin red-faced man with a mustache approached me.

"You must be Greg! I'm Mr. Niles, the host of 'Everything to Lose.' Please have a seat on set and we'll get started!"

I sat down on a stool in front of the camera. It seemed odd that there was no crew operating the equipment, but I pushed my doubts aside. Mr. Niles stood behind the podium and began to ask me general questions about my life, which I answered.

破釜沉舟

這真是幸運到有點難以置信。我一直為金錢問題煩惱，然後有一天，我收到了一封信，它可以幫我解決所有問題。

恭喜！您已被選中成為遊戲節目「破釜沉舟」的參賽者。勝出者將會獲得巨額現金獎勵！請於 2019 年 5 月 31 日前跟我們聯絡……

下面是他們的地址。我合乎情理地抱持懷疑態度，可是作為一個被債務纏身的醫學生，我真的很需要這筆錢。

我根據他們提供的地址，來到一個位於荒廢城鎮裏的大型倉庫。我在裏面閒逛著，才發現有一些攝影機，面向著一個很基本的場景。一個留著小鬍子、紅著臉的瘦男子向我走近。

「你一定是 Greg 吧！我是 Niles 先生，是 『破釜沉舟』的主持人。請過來坐下吧，我們很快就會開始了！」

我坐在鏡頭前的凳子上。沒有工作人員操作著這些攝影器材，好像有點奇怪，但我還是把疑慮拋諸腦後。Niles 先生站在講台後面，開始問起一些關於我生活的普通問題，我也如實回答了。

"Now, Greg, onto your challenge! For $200,000, you must... lose 50lbs by the last day of June!"

My stomach lurched. 50lbs in a month? Was that even possible? I decided that I had to at least try. The idea of having that much money was too alluring. Besides, as a short guy, my 180lbs of weight made me look stumpy, so I supposed being that trim might be nice.

I accepted the challenge, and Mr. Niles gave me instructions on how to e-mail him my weigh-in photo.

"If I don't receive an adequate photo by June 30th, the challenge is off and you'll have no chance to compete again," he warned.

I agonized over how to lose that weight. I did countless Google searches and immediately put myself on a cleanse that consisted of water, lemon, and cayenne pepper. But I couldn't stand that for more than a week and I had no energy to exercise. I tried a diet that allowed one vegan smoothie during the day and then 3oz of protein with veggies for dinner. But the weight simply wasn't coming off fast enough. I had horrible anxiety watching that $200,000 slip through my fingers. That kind of money was enough to put my life back on track.

「好吧，Greg，現在宣布你的挑戰任務！獎金二十萬美元，你必須……在六月的最後一天前減掉五十磅！」

我的胃猛地一跳。一個月五十磅？有可能嗎？不過我決定至少也嘗試一下。獎金金額實在太誘人了。除此以外，我個頭不高，一百八十磅的體重使我看起來矮墩墩的，所以我認為這次讓自己清減一點可能會更好。

我接受了挑戰，接著 Niles 先生便教了我如何把秤重的認證照片電郵給他。

「要是我在六月三十日前還沒有收到合格的照片，挑戰就會宣告失敗，而你將無法再次參加比賽。」他警告說。

我為了減輕體重絞盡腦汁，在 Google 搜索了無數次有關減重的資訊，又馬上實行了「身體淨化計劃」，每天只喝水、只吃檸檬和卡宴辣椒，來幫助排毒。但我只維持了一個星期就無法堅持下去了，因為我沒有多餘的力氣去做運動。接著我嘗試了另一種餐單，在白天可喝一杯素食冰沙，在晚餐時可以吃三盎司蛋白質和蔬菜。可是體重還是降得不夠快。我仿佛看見那二十萬美元正從我的指縫中溜走，想到這裏，我實在焦慮得要命。那筆錢足以讓我的生活重回正軌啊。

Then, one night while I was lying awake in bed, the solution came to me.

It was June 30th and I was proudly emailing my weigh-in photo to Mr. Niles, the scale showing my weight at 130lbs on the dot. Exactly one hour later, there was a knock at my door. I hobbled over and opened it to find him standing there.

"Congratulations, Greg! Just wanted to deliver your reward for a job well done."

He shook my hand as his eyes examined my crutches, my bandaged stump, and my one remaining leg. An enormous grin stretched across his red face. He handed me the check, showing $200,000 made out to my name.

"Job well done indeed."

有天晚上，我躺在床上，睡不著，卻突然想到了解決方案。

到了六月三十日，我自豪地把自己的秤重照片電郵給 Niles 先生，照片中的磅顯示著，我的體重落在一百三十磅的刻度上。剛好過了一個小時後，我家門口傳來了敲門聲。我一瘸一拐地走過去打開門，看見他站在門前。

「恭喜你啊，Greg！你幹得很漂亮，我是過來給你獎勵的。」

他跟我握手的同時，雙眼正打量著我的拐杖、用繃帶包紮著的殘肢和剩下的那條腿。他紅著的臉上展露出一個大得可怕的笑容。他把支票遞給我，上面寫著二十萬美元，還有我的名字。

「確實幹得很漂亮呢。」

A Cure for Depression

Suzanne watched as the agent sorted through the photographs of her late husband.

"Your husband looks very happy in these pictures," said Agent Carlisle. **"I take it his chip was working well before it malfunctioned?"**

Suzanne nodded. "Yeah, it seemed like the implant had really done the trick up til that point," she said. "Before the procedure, he'd get these really bad bouts of depression that would last for days, sometimes weeks at a time. We thought the chip had cured him until—well, you know..."

Agent Carlisle gave a solemn nod. "Yes, we were all pretty startled by the news of your husband's suicide."

Suzanne got up to pour them each a cup of herbal tea, then rejoined Agent Carlisle at the table. Dark bags were beginning to form under Suzanne's eyes, and she seemed too young for the gray streaks beginning to show up around her scalp.

"It's weird," Suzanne started, "I totally bought in to the idea that the implant was foolproof. Yet when Jack killed himself— for whatever strange, subconscious reason—it didn't startle me that much, you know?"

抑鬱症治療

Suzanne 看著探員在整理自己已故丈夫的照片。

「在這些照片中看來，你丈夫很開心啊。」Carlisle 探員說道：「**他的晶片在發生故障之前，應該是一切正常的，我這樣推測正確嗎？**」

Suzanne 點點頭。「沒錯，植入晶片後好像真的有些幫助。」她說：「進行手術之前，他的抑鬱症會經常發作，而且每次都很嚴重，也會持續數天，有時甚至幾星期。我們都以為晶片已經治癒了他，直至，呃，你知道吧……」

Carlisle 探員嚴肅地點了點頭。「是的，收到你丈夫自殺的消息時，我們都非常震驚。」

Suzanne 起身給自己和 Carlisle 各倒了一杯花草茶，然後回到桌子繼續她們的對話。Suzanne 的黑眼圈越來越深了，幾撮銀灰色的髮絲若隱若現，與她年輕的模樣實在不太匹配。

「這不尋常啊。」Suzanne 開口說：「我還以為植入晶片會是個萬無一失的方法。要是 Jack 自殺時，他是因為腦海裏出現其他奇怪的想法，或是一些想自毀的潛意識驅使也好，也不會像現在的這個原因讓我如此驚訝啊，你知道嗎？」

Agent Carlisle sipped on her tea. "Yeah, I suppose that is a bit odd—"

"You married, Agent Carlisle?" Suzanne interrupted. The suddenness of this question caught the agent off-guard; she shook her head.
"Twice-divorced, I'm afraid."

Suzanne's lips elevated into a weak smile. "It's a funny thing, marriage," she said. "Verbal communication eventually becomes a secondary thing. After a while you become hard-wired to your spouse's psyche, for better or for worse."

Agent Carlisle grinned. "Yeah, I know the feeling."

Tears suddenly began to streak down Suzanne's face. She dabbed her eyes with a paper napkin, then stared Agent Carlisle right in the eyes.

"Those last three days were hell for him," Suzanne said, her voice trembling as she fought back tears. "He never spoke a word to me about it, but I could tell. A spouse can always tell."

Agent Carlisle glanced at her watch. She was running late for her next interview. Rising from her chair, she offered Suzanne

Carlisle 探員呷了口茶，「是的，我也覺得這有點不太尋常呢⋯⋯」

「Carlisle 探員，你結婚了嗎？」Suzanne 打斷道。這個突如其來的問題讓探員防不勝防，她搖了搖頭。
「我離過兩次婚。」

Suzanne 的嘴唇彎成了淡淡的微笑。「是一件有趣的事情呢，婚姻。」她說：「口頭交流最終會變成次要的事情。再過一會兒，無論怎樣也好，你和配偶都會變得同床異夢般疏離。」

Carlisle 探員咧嘴一笑：「是的，我明白這種感覺。」

Suzanne 的臉突然劃過一行行淚痕。她用紙巾輕擦了眼睛，然後盯進 Carlisle 探員的雙眼。

「最後那三天對他來說真是太糟糕了。」Suzanne 說著，聲音因為強忍眼淚而顫抖。「他從來沒有對我說過，關於那件事的一切，但我看得出來。配偶總能看得出來。」

Carlisle 探員瞥了手錶一眼，她快要趕不及下一個面談了。從椅子站起來後，Carlisle 探員向 Suzanne 投以一個同情的表情。

a look of expressed sympathy.

"You've been very helpful today, ma'am. Thank you for your time, considering the circumstances," said the agent, heading towards the front door.

"There are others, aren't there?" Suzanne asked. The agent paused as she reached for the doorknob. "A manufacturing error like **that would've affected more people than just my husband, right**?"

Agent Carlisle shook her head. "We've marked your husband's suicide down as an isolated incident. This isn't a consumer matter," she said bluntly, then turned the doorknob.

As the agent walked down the driveway, she wondered why she'd lied to the widow. Of course that chip hadn't been the only one to malfunction, and by the time the story broke there would be millions more.

Agent Carlisle scratched the small scar above her right ear, then got in her car.

「你今天提供的資訊對我們的調查很有幫助。感謝你寶貴的時間，也感謝你考慮到各方面的情況。」探員邊説邊走向前門。

「還有其他人嗎？」Suzanne問道。當時探員已碰到了門把，聽見 Suzanne 的話，她頓了一下。「這種出廠時的技術錯誤不只影響到我丈夫吧，**還有很多其他受害者吧？**」

Carlisle 探員搖了搖頭。「我們已經將你丈夫的自殺標記為個別事件。這不是消費者的問題。」她直言不諱地説，然後扭開了門把。

當探員沿著車道走下去時，她不知自己為何要對那個寡婦撒謊。當然，那個晶片並不是唯一一個出現故障的晶片，當這個消息傳出去時，早已有數百萬個受害人了。

Carlisle 探員舉手抓了抓她右耳上方的小疤痕，然後上了自己的車。

That Day Had Teeth

"It's not a story I always like talking about. I'll do it quick. I linger too long and... I can get worked up.

It was summer. Morning, early - maybe five a.m. I dressed quickly for work, kissed both of you and your mother goodbye.

Outside, in front of the car, I stopped and looked at the sky. It was completely birdless. Quiet. The pale, urine yellow of early morning summer. Little bits of indifferent clouds. Alien clouds. Strips of rotten gauze. It felt like the day was primed and ready for something, some kind of event. It had teeth.

Driving to work felt like a slow-motion nightmare. No cars on the road, no people, no birds. To this day, I... just where were the birds? I looked and looked but all there was was that fever-yellow sky cloying and watching. Those ugly clouds like claw marks in the sky. You'll think I'm crazy. No, I'm fine; I'll carry on.

So, **in the distance I saw a car on the hard shoulder.** Its hazards were on.

淡黃的一天

「其實我不太喜歡説這個故事，所以我會儘快把它説完。我磨蹭得太久了⋯⋯我可以提起勁來的。

那是一個夏天的早上，很早──大概是清晨五點吧。我醒來後飛快地換好衣服準備上班，跟你倆和你倆的母親吻別後便出門了。

到了外面，站在車子前，我停了下來，看著天空。一隻鳥兒也沒有，安靜得很。夏天清晨獨有的淡黃天色，零散而事不關己的雲朵在旁點綴。雲朵酷似一絲絲的爛紗布般，奇形怪狀的。那天世界好像準備好迎接某些事情似的；那天仿佛有股莫名的力量控制著我似的。

開車上班活像一個慢動作的噩夢。路上沒有車、沒有人，也沒有鳥。直到今天，我⋯⋯到底鳥兒到哪裏去了？我看來看去，卻只見泛黃得發膩的天空在監視著我。那些醜陋的雲在天空中像一道道爪痕。你覺得我瘋了嗎？不，我沒事。我繼續説下去了。

然後，我看見遠處的緊急停車處，**有輛正閃著危險警告燈的車子停了在那邊。**

As I passed, I looked over. Front seats empty, two little girls in the back. Pig-tails, deep brown eyes. They watched me pass. They had dolls. Your age back then, maybe younger. I thought of you both and worried for them.

Before I could think, I saw a man, must have been the father, I thought, walking up the side of the road, carrying a canister. Getting petrol. I knew the station was not too far a walk from here, maybe ten minutes. He looked tired.

I thought maybe I should stop and give him a lift. Maybe.

The funny thing is - I knew, I somehow just knew, if I got out of my car, under that yellow sky, I'd bounce like a spaceman. That's what the air was like - like I was on another planet. I'd bounce, and all would be quiet, and the birds would cease existing forever and I'd never hear them sing again. But I didn't tell myself that. I told myself I'd be late for work.

So I didn't stop. I kept going. I just kept going.

Two days later there was a story in the newspaper; I read the headline and my breath caught in my throat. Everything turned yellow.

我駛過它旁邊時，往車子裏面看了看。前排座位是空的，後面座位有兩個小女孩。她們綁著小辮子，有著深褐色的眼睛。她們望著我在旁駛過，手中還抱著娃娃。她們跟那時的你們差不多年紀吧，可能更小一點。看到她們，我想起了你們，也不禁為她們憂心。

我還未來得及思考，眼前就出現了一個男人，他想必一定是她們的父親吧。他在路邊走著，拿著一個罐子，裏面裝滿了汽油。我知道油站距離這裡不遠，大概十分鐘路程而已，可是他看上來累透了。

我想也許我應該停下來幫他一把。也許。

有趣的是，我知道，我有預感，如果我下車，在那黃色的天空下，我就會像個太空人般飄浮起來。那時的空氣讓我覺得自己身處在另一個星球上——我會飄浮起來，萬物都會變得安靜，鳥兒將不復存在，而我再也聽不到牠們歌唱了。但我沒有跟自己說這些話，我只告訴自己我上班快遲到了。

所以我沒有停下來，我繼續往前走，一直往前走。

兩天後，報紙刊登了一篇報道；看到了標題，我幾乎窒息了。一切都變成黃色了。

A man had fallen asleep in his truck - poor, overworked bastard, killed himself later I think - and ploughed into that car with the little girls and their dolls. Swerved right off the road. Killed them instantly.

I dropped the paper, found you both playing, and held you close. I'm not ashamed to say I cried. I didn't tell your mother why.

Well, now, I think about the father sometimes. Where he is now. Whether he had more children. Whether his wife stood by him. But most of all I wonder if he's alive to dream, and if he dreams of the yellow too."

有個男人駕著卡車時打瞌睡了（他應該是個因工作過勞的可憐蟲，我猜他後來應該自殺了），向女孩們那輛車直衝過去，把她們的車子撞翻了，更拋出了路壆。那對小女孩當場死亡。

我把報紙掉到地上，看見你們都在玩，但我還是把你們緊抱在懷裏。我哭了，但我並不感到羞恥。我甚至沒告訴你們的母親我在哭甚麼。

到了現在，我有時還是會想起那個父親，不知道他現在在哪裏呢，他會不會多生幾個孩子呢，他的妻子有否守在他身邊呢……但我最常想起的是，如果他還活著，仍能做夢的話，不知道他有否夢見那些淡黃的一切呢。」

The Pointing Girl

I have seen ghosts my whole life. When I was a little girl my parents sent me to a shrink, but no matter what drug or council I was given, they never went away.

Out of every ghost I have seen throughout my life, there is one I will never forget. The Pointing Girl.

It was Valentine's Day 1998, and I was sixteen. By this point I had learnt to remain calm whenever I saw something, no matter how chilling. That's what I did when I saw her.

I was waiting for the school bus while she stood across the street. She was a small girl with long blonde curls, wearing a cute polka dot dress. If it wasn't for the fact her neck was wide open and she wasn't creepily staring and pointing at me, I might have found her adorable.

At school, the first half of the day went as usual. I walked to class by myself, I sat by myself and then I ate lunch by myself. But something new happened before last period. I found a Valentine's Day card in my locker.

At first, I thought it was a joke, but it was signed "Your secret admirer, **JB**." I knew right away it was Jeremy Benson, he would always smile at me, and I would always blush.

指劃女孩

我從出生以來就能看見幽靈。當我還是小女孩時，父母就帶過我去看精神科醫生，但不管醫生處方了甚麼藥物給我也好，跟我輔導過多少次也好，幽靈們都不曾離開過。

在我一生中見過那麼多幽靈當中，有一個讓我永遠不能忘懷的幽靈，那就是指劃女孩。

回溯到 1998 年的情人節，那時我十六歲。當時的我已經學會了無論看到多麼驚嚇的事物，都要保持冷靜。這也就是我看到她時的反應。

那時我在等校車，她就站在對面的街道上。她是個小女孩，長著一把金色的長捲髮，穿著可愛的圓點連衣裙。要不是因為她脖子有一個超大的缺口，而且詭異地盯著我、指向我的話，我可能也會覺得她很可愛。

到了學校，前半天像往常一樣，我獨自走到課室，獨自坐著，然後獨自吃午飯。但是在上最後一課之前，有新劇情展開了——我的儲物櫃裏有一張情人節賀卡。

起初我還以為那只是開玩笑的，但下款的簽署寫著「你的秘密崇拜者，JB。」我立刻就知道寄件人是 Jeremy Benson，他常常對我微笑，而我總是會臉紅起來。

During last period I shared a class with Jeremy, so I sat next to him. To my surprise, he talked to me. Soon we were laughing and gossiping. It was mostly about our new creepy substitute, Mr Banks, who had a habit of wheezing whenever he was happy. We both found it hilarious.

It was nearing the end of class when I spotted her again. Through the window I saw her on the football field. **She was shambling towards me with her arm stretched out in front of her, pointing at me.** Chills went down my spine, and I had to look away.

When I got home I told my parents all about my day and I even showed them the card. They were both so happy for me.

I finally felt normal.

Unfortunately, the feeling didn't last. Before bed, while closing my curtains, there she was again. **Standing in our driveway, pointing up at me.** I quickly pulled them shut and rushed under my covers.

Later that night, I was awoken by the sound of shuffling. I rubbed the sleep from my eyes and that's when I saw her.

我跟 Jeremy 一起上最後一節課，所以我坐在他旁邊。令我
驚訝的是，他跟我說話了。很快我們就聊得很高興、很開懷。
話題主要圍繞我們那個怪異的新代課老師，Banks 先生，他
有個小毛病，他快樂的時候會喘氣。我和 Jeremy 都覺得他
這樣很搞笑。

快下課的時候，我再次看到了她。透過教室的窗戶，我看到
她站了在足球場上。**她蹣跚地向我的方向走近，然後手臂伸
到前方，指著我。**我嚇得打了個冷顫，不得不把目光移開。

回到家時，我跟父母訴說當天在學校發生過的事，甚至向他
們展示了那張賀卡。他們都很替我高興。

我終於覺得自己是個正常人了。

不幸的是，這個感覺很快就消退了。躺上床前，我正打算關
上窗簾時，她又來了。**她站在我家的車道上，指著我。**我迅
速將窗簾關上，然後衝到床上用被子蓋著自己。

那晚，我被一些曳足而行的聲音吵醒了。我揉了揉自己的睡
眼，張開眼就看到了她。

She was standing in the corner of my room, pointing. I sat up in shock as I realised what she was doing. **She wasn't pointing at me, she was pointing under my bed.** Then I heard the wheezing.

I ran screaming out of my room.

Not long after I found myself on the street, watching as the police dragged **Mr. Jonathan Banks** out of my house.

That's when I stopped being afraid of the dead... the living are far more terrifying.

她站在我房間的角落，指劃著。當我意識到她的用意時，我震驚地坐起來。**她不是指著我，而是指著我的床下。**然後我聽見了喘氣聲。

我尖叫著跑出房間。

不久後，我發現自己在街上，看著警察把 Jonathan Banks 先生拖出我家。

那時開始，我就不再害怕死者……生者才更加可怕。

The Sting Still Hurt

"Stay near me, Yanny," I said, trying my hardest to keep my voice calm. The soft echoes rebounded around the massive cavern. My scythe was poised for battle, gleaming with the blood of the demons felled. "We're almost at the gates."

Yanny nodded. The journey had been taxing for her; mentally, she was not a very strong girl. "Please," she said weakly, almost whispering, "protect me."

On cue, a massive red scorpion sprung up, stinger slamming straight into where Yanny would have been, had I not shoved her out of the way.

"Run!" I shouted at her, and engaged the demon.

My scythe flashed as it spun through the air, hissing wherever it found a chink in the beast's armour. From the corner of my eye, I saw Yanny running blindly away from us. The Gates were a few hundred metres away, **a welcome conclusion at the end of a thirty-day odyssey.**

I slashed off a pincer, ignoring the shriek of the monster, and raced towards Yanny.

蛇蠍心腸

「跟緊我啊，Yanny⋯⋯」我盡力讓自己的聲音保持平靜地說道。溫和的回聲在巨大的洞穴裏迴響著。我的鐮刀已經蓄勢待發，準備好隨時戰鬥，刀刃上隱約地閃現著那些被我打倒的魔獸的血液。「我們快要到達大門了。」

Yanny點了點頭。這段旅程對她來說太費勁了。而在精神層面上，她也不是一個非常堅強的女孩。「求求你⋯⋯」虛弱的她幾乎是用氣聲的道：「保護我⋯⋯」

就在此時，一隻巨大的紅蠍子突然出現，蠍子的毒刺猛地撞向了Yanny原來的位置，要是我沒有把她推開的話，她已經受襲了。

「快跑！」我對她大喊，然後與那隻魔獸開戰。

我的鐮刀在空中飛舞時閃閃發亮，揮向魔獸盔甲上的每個縫隙時，發出嘶嘶聲。我眼角瞥到Yanny頭也不回地跑走了。我們離大門只有幾百米遠，**這場歷時三十天、漫長而驚險的旅程快要來到尾聲了。**

砍掉了蠍子的一隻螯針後，我無視它的尖叫聲，向Yanny直奔過去。

"We're almost there!" she screamed, half-crying, half-laughing. Most of them end up like this at the end, torn between accepting their fate and fighting for their destiny. I had always admired this about mortals - with a life so short, they could only fight for their destiny. Us, we've seen fates longer than time, endings where beginnings have yet to start. There was no destiny for us.

We were twenty seconds from the gate now. Fifteen. Te-

A huge pressure slammed into me from behind and I was pinned against the wall of the cavern. Grimacing, I grabbed on to a rock, trying to resist the pull of the scorpion.

"Help me!" I cried to Yanny, who had frozen from the shock. My scythe, which had fallen by her feet, captured every bit of fear in her eyes. "Cut off its pincer!"

The scorpion was now positioned to sting. Murder was evident in its eyes; with a stinger that size, it didn't even need poison. I might be Death, but wounds were still wounds.

Yanny took one last look at me, then said the one thing that always haunted me no matter how many times I heard it.

"I'm sorry. Thank you."

「我們快到了！」她半哭半笑地叫喊著。大多數人最後的結局也是像這樣的，在認命和抗命之間左右為難。我一直很羨慕凡人——生命如此短暫，他們只能選擇抗命。而我們，我們觀看命運所花的光陰比時間還久遠，一切還未開始便已看到了結局。我們沒有所謂的命運。

我們現在距離大門只有二十秒鐘，十五，十……

突然，有股巨大的壓力從後面撞向我，我被釘在洞穴的牆上。面目猙獰的我抓住一塊岩石，試圖與蠍子的力量抗衡。

「救我！」我向 Yanny 喊道，她震驚得呆住了。我的鐮刀掉了在她腳邊，刀刃反射出她充滿恐懼的眼神。「砍掉它的螫針！」

蠍子現在已經作出了舉起毒刺的攻擊姿態。牠眼裏充滿殺意；以那根毒刺的大小，沒有毒素也夠殺傷力了。就算我是死神也好，但傷口仍然會是傷口。

Yanny 看了我最後一眼，然後説了一句話，那是無論我聽過多少次，還是會讓我懊惱不已的一句話。

「我很抱歉，謝謝你了。」

She turned and ran towards the pearly white Gates, towards the urgently beckoning winged angel that stood there. The pressure around my midsection released as she made it through, never even turning around to look at the one being who had protected her throughout the journey.

I picked up my scythe and sighed, watching as the Gates chained themselves shut and slowly bled to red. I recognized the screams of Yanny. I recognized the screams of all the other people who had abandoned me to the scorpion, who had already regrown its lost limbs and was happily escorting me back to the entrance. When a happy ending is in sight, few would risk themselves to *save* another.

Selfish. Selfish, the whole lot of you.

她轉身跑向珍珠白色的大門，跑向那個站在大門外、不斷向她招手的翼天使。我望著她穿過了大門，她甚至沒有轉過頭來看看在整個旅程中保護她的這個人，但我似乎放下了心頭大石。

我拾起了鐮刀，嘆了口氣，看著大門自行關上了，接著漸漸因染血而變成紅色。我認出了 Yanny 的尖叫聲，也認出了那些同樣把我捨棄了、讓蠍子刺向我的人的尖叫聲。此時蠍子已經重新長回了那些被我砍掉的手腳，並欣然地護送我回到入口處。當一個大團圓結局在眼前出現時，很少人會冒險捨身拯救其他人。

自私，自私鬼，你們全部都是自私鬼。

I Reported a Missing Person

"911, what's your emergency?"

I hesitated on the phone, all of a sudden a little shy. I had never called 911 before, and talking to new people always makes me antsy. I wished Tom were there… but, of course, that's why I was calling. I took a deep breath, cleared my throat, and answered.

"Hi, um… my name is Terry Millerson and I'd like to report a missing person. Tom Smith."

"And how long has… I'm sorry, **what was that name?**"
"Tom Smith."

"No, no - I mean, **what did you say your name was?**"

I sighed impatiently. "My name is Terry Millerson. Look, Tom hasn't been home for over twelve hours. That may not seem like a lot, but that's a very long time for him. He never goes away that long without telling me when he'll be back. So can you just…"

"Ms. Millerson, can you tell us your address?"

I paused, uncertainty creeping in. "Why do you want to know my address?"

匯報失蹤人口

「911 報案中心，你有甚麼緊急案件需要申報？」

我拿著話筒，有點遲疑，又突然有點害羞。這是我第一次打電話報案，而且跟陌生人談話總是讓我很不自在。我真希望 Tom 能在我身邊呢，不過這正是我報案的原因。

我深深吸了一口氣，清清喉嚨，然後回答：「你好，呃⋯⋯我叫 Terry Millerson，我想匯報一個失蹤人口，他叫 Tom Smith。」

「他失蹤了多⋯⋯不好意思，**那個名字是？**」
「Tom Smith。」

「不是不是，我是指，**你剛剛說你的名字是甚麼？**」

我不耐煩地嘆了口氣：「我的名字是 Terry Millerson。聽好了，Tom 已經有十二小時沒有回家了，雖然聽起來時間不長，但這情況對他來說已經很久了。他從來不會離開那麼久，而且沒有跟我說甚麼時候會回來，所以能請你⋯⋯」

「Millerson 小姐，可以告訴我你的地址嗎？」

我頓了一頓，不安感湧現。「你為甚麼想要知道我的地址？」

"Ms. Millerson, do you know where you are?"

I covered up my embarrassment with a bit of bluster. "At home, obviously."

"And what address is that?"

I lost my patience. "I don't know, okay?! What does it matter? Look, just find Tom so I know he's going to be okay, you got that?"

"Ms. Millerson, please tell us where you are, your parents are very worried, we are coming to find you-"

At that moment, Tom walked in. I breathed a sigh of relief and hung up the phone just as he spied me.

His face went red, but I didn't mind.

"What the fuck are you doing? How did you get up here?"

I smiled brightly at him. "Tom, there you are. I was so worried when you didn't come home! I thought something had happened to you! You left the basement door unlocked. You never leave the door unlocked. Is everything okay?"

「Millerson 小姐，小姐你知道自己在哪裏嗎？」

為了掩飾自己的尷尬，我大聲嚷道：「在家啊，不用問也知道啦！」

「那請問地址是甚麼？」

我的耐性已經耗盡了。「我不知道，可以嗎？這有甚麼關係？你聽著，快點幫我找回 Tom，讓我知道他沒有事就好了，你明白嗎？」

「Millerson 小姐，請告訴我們你的位置，你的父母很擔心，我們會來找你──」

此際，Tom 回來了，我鬆了一口氣，可是生怕會被他發現，我迅速掛了電話。

他的臉漲紅了，可是我不介意。

「你在這裏幹甚麼鬼？你怎麼會上來這裏？」

我向他展露燦爛的笑容：「你回來了！你這麼久還沒有回家，我很擔心你！我以為你發生甚麼事了呢！你沒有鎖上地下室

Tom closed his eyes and took a deep breath. "Did you tell the police where you are?"

"No, sir. I just asked them to find you for me. Did you talk to them?"

He paused a moment, then opened his eyes and smiled at me. "No, but I'll be sure to tell them that I'm safe and not to worry about it."

I beamed at him as he took my manacled hands in his, running his thumbs across the metal. He always does that when he's being sweet. I didn't like it at first but I love it now. **I love a lot of things about Tom now.**

"Come on, sweetie, let's get you back downstairs, hm?"
"Yes, sir," I said happily as he ushered me towards the basement.

就出門了，你從來不會忘記上鎖，沒發生甚麼事吧？」

Tom 閉上眼睛，深呼吸了一下，問我：「你有跟警察説你在哪嗎？」

「沒有，先生，我只是請求他們替我找你，你有跟他們談話嗎？」

Tom 頓了片刻，張開眼向我微笑説：「沒有，但我一定會告訴他們我很安全，不用擔心我。」

他牽起我那雙戴著鐐銬的手，用拇指滑過我手上的金屬，我報以微笑。他跟我示好時總是會這樣做。我一開始並不喜歡，但我現在卻愛上了。**我愛上很多有關 Tom 的事情。**

「過來吧，親愛的，回到樓下吧，好嗎？」
「好的，先生。」我高興地回應，然後跟他一起走回地下室。

Respect the World
别 小 看 世 界

This is What You Get
When You Mess With Us

I watch the two young men creep along the silent subway station, eyes focused on their target. They approach a frail elderly man who is waiting for the train. There is not another soul around.

The two men come at the senior citizen from both sides, one of them grabbing his arms, the other holding a knife against his stomach and demanding his wallet.

The terrified old man obliges, muttering pleas to not hurt him. One of the young men snatches the wallet, looks through it, pockets it, and then without even hesitating, shoves the old man onto the tracks.

They dart away, laughing, as lights illuminate the tunnel, indicating that a train is approaching. The old man lies unconscious on the tracks, unaware that he is about to be decimated.

I follow the young men. They cannot be older than 21. They have their hoods up to hide their faces. They always wear hoodies when they do this.

I know because I've seen them do this same routine three other times. They rob someone who is waiting for a train alone late at night and then shove them onto the tracks to die.

罪有應得

在夜闌人靜的火車站裏，我看著兩個年輕男子鬼鬼祟祟的，凝視著他們的目標人物——一個正在等車、瘦骨嶙峋的老伯，月台上再沒有其他人了。

他們兩個從左右兩邊走向老伯，一個抓著他的手臂，另一個用刀子架著他的肚子，要他交出錢包。

嚇壞了的老伯乖乖服從，只呢喃著叫他們不要傷害自己。其中一名年輕男子接過錢包，左翻右翻，掏空了裏面的東西後，絲毫沒有遲疑地，把老伯推下了路軌。

他們大笑著跑走了，與此同時，光線照亮了隧道，這表示有火車正在駛進車站。老伯意識模糊地躺在路軌，察覺不到他將要命喪黃泉了。

我跟蹤著那兩個年輕男子，我肯定他們還未滿二十一歲。他們把兜帽蓋著臉，他們幹這回事的時候，總是穿著連帽衛衣。

這次是我第四次目睹他們這樣做了，所以我很清楚他們的衣著。他們會對那些在夜裏獨自等車的人下手，然後把他們推到路軌殺掉他們。

"Old man was a fuckin' idiot to be carrying this much cash with him. Doesn't he know there are dangerous people out there?" says the one in the grey sweatshirt, once they are far away from the scene of the crime. He roars with laughter.

"You sure we're not gonna get caught? Karma's a bitch," says the one in the black sweatshirt. "A big old fat fucking bitch."

"Fuck you and your karma. We got nothing to worry about."

The next time they're planning to strike, I'm there again.

This time, they're targeting a small young woman, anxiously waiting for her train around 4am. They lurk up to her, hoods up, and that's when I make my move.

They don't see me, of course, but they feel me.

In a second, I'm directly behind them. I shove them violently and their bodies clatter onto the tracks. They fall so hard that I hear bones breaking upon the impact. They look up, utterly disoriented. The woman runs away to get help. **I watch as the train lights appear from deep within the tunnel.**

「那個老伯真他媽的笨！竟然帶著這麼多現金。難道不知道街上有很多壞人嗎？」他們離案發現場一段距離後，身穿灰色囚衣的小伙子邊說邊大笑。

「你肯定我們不會被抓嗎？報應這回事很靈驗喔⋯⋯」黑色囚衣的小子回應：「而且那些報應總是他媽的惡毒啊！」

「去你的報應，我們沒有甚麼好擔心的。」

當他們準備再次行動時，我也在附近。

現在是凌晨四時左右，他們這次的目標是一個正不安地等著車、嬌小的年輕女子。他們戴起兜帽走近她，然後是時候換我出手了。

他們看不到我，這是理所當然的，但他們感覺到我的存在。

下一秒，我已在他們的身後。我狠狠地把他們推下路軌，他們呼地掉了下去，骨頭應聲斷裂。他們望了上來，眼神迷茫。那個女子馬上跑開了求救。**火車的燈正漸漸照亮著隧道，而我正在袖手旁觀。**

Miraculously, the conductor spots the men on the tracks and tries to slam on the brakes. Of course it's too late, and the train glides over their bodies. The sounds of crunching and screaming echo in the subway station.

Once the train has sailed passed their bodies, I force it to reverse. The conductor is confused; he doesn't understand why the train is moving on its own. The train slithers back over the crushed deformed bodies of the young men, demolishing them for a second time.

It's not always easy, this job. Sometimes I get carried away, but I can't help it. After all, **I just absolutely hate it when someone calls me a bitch.**

出乎意料地，車長看到了路軌上有兩名男子，嘗試急剎火車。可惜已經太遲了，火車已經輾過了他們的身體。嘎吱的撕裂聲和尖叫聲響遍整個火車站。

當那輛火車駛過他們的身體時，我強行把它退回去。車長很疑惑，他不明白為甚麼火車會自己動。火車再一次向後移動，再次蹂躪年輕男子早已支離破碎的身體，進一步摧毀它們。

這個崗位不容易當啊，很多時我也只是被牽著鼻子走，甚麼也改變不了。**可是我真的超討厭別人說我很惡毒啊。**

The Race Goes On Forever

I'm whimpering as I sit on the uncomfortable motorcycle seat. To my left, someone is crying openly. The sound is drowned out by the announcer, yet again signaling the beginning of the race that goes on forever.

None of us know how we got here. The longer we stay, the more we forget about who we were.

Against my will, my hand releases the throttle. I fly down the cobblestones. The bouncing is so rough I know it'll bruise me, but that's the least of my worries here.

Whenever they summon us, we race. When they don't need us, we go away somewhere – I don't know exactly where or how. It's a dark, quiet place, like going to sleep.

I crest a hill and my stomach drops when I see the sheer cliff faces with no guardrail. Something collides with the woman next to me, sending her screaming into the abyss.

I think I used to work at a school.

I hear thunder and then my body is burning with pain. I press on, my face grim, trying to ignore the agonizing bursts of electricity that dance across my skin, causing my muscles to jump and twitch erratically.

永無止境的比賽

坐在不舒服的摩托車座椅上，我低聲抽泣著。在我的左邊有人大聲哭鬧著。廣播員的聲音蓋過了哭聲，這代表著這個永無止境的比賽即將開始了。

無人知道為何我們會來到這裏。我們留在這裏的時間愈長，便愈難想起自己到底是誰。

我的手不由自主地鬆開了節流閥，向那些鵝卵石俯衝過去。路上顛簸得肯定會把我全身弄傷，但這是我在這裏最不擔心的事。

只要他們召喚我們，我們便要比賽；但當他們不需要我們的時候，我不知道他們走到哪裏或是如何離開的，總之他們就會走到別處。而我們則會留在一個又黑又靜的地方，像睡著了的感覺。

我到達了山頂，當我看到陡峭卻沒有護欄的懸崖時，我的胃開始翻滾了。旁邊的女子撞到了些甚麼，尖叫聲和她一同掉下深淵。

我想我以前是在學校工作的。

我聽見了雷聲，接著我的身體便燃燒起來，並帶來劇痛。面

I'm so close to the end. If I win, I win the only thing worth having in this place – the briefest moment of reprieve before they send me back to sleep.

The man in front of me is the only thing in my way. **I consider my options and fire my weapon.**

The explosion is the loudest I've heard since coming here, and I can hear the man screaming as his skin melts and bones shatter. I zoom past, trying not to look. I know he will regenerate, but that doesn't save you from experiencing the pain. You feel everything, every crack, every scrape, every impact.

I cross the finish line.

Lee and Katie rushed downstairs. After a long day at school, they were ready to unwind a little.

The TV flickered to life. Cheerful music streamed from its speakers.

Mario Kart! Press A to continue...

容扭曲的我繼續向前奔馳，嘗試忽略那些導致我的肌肉跳動和不規則地抽搐、在我的皮膚連環爆發、折騰得要命的電流。

我快要到達終點了，如果我勝出了，就會得到這個地方最具價值的獎品——在他們送我回去睡覺之前，會有一段很短的緩刑時刻。

我面前的障礙物只有一個男子，**我選好了武器，然後發射。**

這是我待在這裏以來聽過最響亮的爆炸聲，還伴隨著那個男子因皮膚融掉和骨頭粉碎而發出的慘叫聲。我飛越了他，盡量不去看他。我知道他會再生的，可是那些痛楚是無可避免的。每次骨裂、每次擦傷、每次撞擊，一切苦難你都會確切感覺到的。

我衝過了終點線。

Lee 和 Katie 跑下樓梯，經過一整天上學的勞碌，是時候放鬆一下了。

電視的屏幕閃爍著光輝，歡樂的背景音樂從揚聲器傳出。

瑪利奧賽車！請按 A 鍵繼續。

Losing at Poker to a Demon

"Please don't do this," I begged the demon.

"Sorry, bro," he said, and went back to the cigarette held between his scarlet fingers.

"I'm begging you," I said helplessly, knowing as soon as the words left my mouth that I was already fucked. "Don't curse me, man."

A mocking laugh erupted from the demon's mouth. The laugh surrounded me, constricting me until I couldn't breathe.

Then it was gone, and the demon flicked the cigarette butt into a puddle. I stood, dumbstruck, as he waved good-bye to me with careless lethargy.

Karen and I got into a fight that very night, practically the moment I got home. I barged through the door so forcefully I made a hole in the drywall. While I was cleaning up, I stepped on our cat's tail, and she clawed right through the leg of my pants in retaliation.

The next day, I awoke to Karen frantically shaking me – I'd forgotten to set my alarm. I had to apologize profusely to my boss and our regional manager for missing the meeting, and **I spent the rest of the day with a cloud hanging over my head.**

惡魔的玩笑

「請不要這樣做……」我向惡魔懇求著。

「對不起啊，兄弟。」他說罷，注意力便回到他那紅色手指間的香煙上。

「我求你了……」我無助地說道，我一開口就知道自己已經徹底地完蛋了，「不要詛咒我吧，兄弟。」

一陣嘲笑聲從惡魔的嘴裏爆發出來。笑聲環繞著我，仿佛要把我壓縮得無法呼吸為止。

笑聲消失了，然後惡魔將煙頭彈到水坑裏。他漫不經心又冷漠地向我揮手告別時，我只懂站在原地發懵。

就在當晚，幾乎在我踏入家門的一刻起，Karen 就和我吵了起來。我橫衝直撞地穿過大門，一股蠻力撞上石膏牆，打出了一個洞。我在清理時，又不小心踩了貓咪的尾巴，牠在我的腿上抓了一下以示報復，力度大得抓穿了我的褲子。

第二天，我在 Karen 的瘋狂搖晃之下醒過來——我忘了設置鬧鐘。由於缺席了會議，我得不斷向老闆和區域經理致歉。**當天餘下的時間裏，我也像是烏雲蓋頂般茫然度過。**

There was unexpected traffic, so it took me an hour to get home instead of twenty minutes – and, again, one of the first things I did when I got there was step on Squeak's tail.

My bad luck continued, and things with Karen soured. She even seemed happy when she was assigned the graveyard shift, meaning we wouldn't see much of each other – the bitch. As I got used to waking up alone, I started wondering what I saw in her to begin with.

She threw me out a month later, when I got arrested for beating up someone at a bar. Whatever. Fuck her. I started living out of my car while I looked for a new place, and did my best to ignore my coworkers' stares and whispers as I started showing up late and unkempt more often.

I ran into my demon friend again, as I was getting thrown out of O'Doull's downtown for the second time that week. I'd blown a presentation that day, and was pretty sure management was preparing to send my ass packing. Time to get drunk.

I crawled to the demon's feet, blubbering. "Can you please lift the curse? Please? My life is in the fucking shitter, man. I learned my lesson, I swear. Please?"

回家路上遇上了交通意外，原本只需二十分鐘的車程，最後卻花了整整一個小時才回到家。而且，我甫回到家，第一件做的事，就是又踩到了 Squeak 的尾巴。

我的厄運持續不散，跟 Karen 的關係也隨之惡化了。當她的工作被分配到凌晨班時，她甚至看起來十分開心，因為這意味著我們不會經常碰到面。真是個婊子。當我習慣獨自醒來時，我開始懷疑自己當初到底喜歡她甚麼。

一個月後，我在酒吧毆打他人被捕，她就把我撇掉了。算了，無所謂，去她的。在找新住宿的同時，我只好暫住在車裏，並且盡我所能地無視同事們的白眼和竊竊私語，因為我遲到及不修邊幅的情況愈趨嚴重了。

當我在一週內第二次被 O'Doull 酒吧趕走時，我再次遇到了那個惡魔朋友。那天的報告演講我搞砸了，而且我頗肯定管理層正準備讓我拔鍋卷席，攆我回家。所以這絕對是個喝得爛醉的好時候呢。

我爬到惡魔的腳邊，放聲大哭地道：「可以請你解除我的詛咒嗎？拜託你了……我就像活在糞桶般，糟糕得要命啊。我發誓，我已經得到應得的教訓了。求求你好嗎？」

The demon's expression was a mixture of surprise, amusement, and condescension. Peals of laughter bubbled out of his throat, and it took him a few minutes before he could even compose himself enough to respond.

"Oh my God," he said, wiping tears from his eyes. "That…. Wow. Thank you. That's the funniest thing that's happened to me in centuries."

I was inebriated enough to be hopeful, but his next words left me speechless and immobilized, kneeling on the grimy sidewalk.

"I never really cursed you, Mike. I was just fucking around."

惡魔的表情混和著驚喜、愉悅，還有一點紆尊降貴。響亮的笑聲又從他的喉嚨裏噴發出來，他花了幾分鐘才平靜下來，作出回應。

「我的天啊！」他擦著眼淚說道：「那真是，哇，謝謝你呢。這是我幾個世紀以來，遇過最有趣的事情呢！」

我醉得竟以為還有一絲希望，但他說出的下一句話讓我無言以對之餘，更跪倒在骯髒的人行道上。

「*Mike，我從來沒有真正詛咒過你。我只是在瞎鬧而已。*」

A Time to Be Born, a Time to Die

Eve was deep inside an empty cave when she found the pocket watch. She almost stepped on it, but jerked her foot back as she saw a glimmer of gold on the rocky surface.

Excited because she had never found anything valuable during her spelunking excursions, she snatched up the watch. When her helmet light illuminated it, she could see it was ancient. To her surprise, she also saw that it was ticking.

That evening, Eve sat in her apartment, examining the pocket watch and trying to figure out how to set it to the correct time.

There was a little button at the top, and **when she pressed it, the hands came to a halt.** That's when she noticed that everything had gone quiet; the TV in the other room was no longer blaring and she didn't hear the usual sounds of honking and kids playing outside.

"Strange," Eve muttered, walking to the window. She peered outside and saw a very strange sight indeed. Every person, animal, and car seemed to have stopped dead in their tracks. Her heart pounded as her brain tried to comprehend what she was seeing.

生有時，死有時

Eve 在一個空洞穴深處，找到了一隻懷錶。她在岩石表面看到金光一閃，就把腿縮了回來，她幾乎踩到那隻懷錶。

Eve 興奮不已，因為她在探險期間，從未發現過任何有價值的東西，於是她抓起了懷錶，用頭盔燈照亮它，發現這是一隻古老的懷錶。令她驚訝的是，懷錶的秒針正在滴答作響。

那天晚上，Eve 回到公寓坐下來，細心檢查著懷錶，並試圖弄清楚如何將它設置到正確的時間。

懷錶頂部有一個小按鈕，當 Eve 按下按鈕時，**懷錶的指針停了下來**。然後 Eve 注意到身邊的一切都變得安靜了——另一個房間的電視不再發出喧鬧聲，平時很嘈吵的喇叭聲，以及孩子們在外面玩耍的聲音也聽不見了。

「奇怪……」Eve 喃喃道，然後走到窗前。望向窗外，確實看到了一個非常奇怪的景象。每個人、每隻動物、每輛汽車好像定格了般一動不動。Eve 的腦袋試圖理解她所看到的一切，心臟也跟著砰砰直跳。

Suddenly, Eve remembered that old *Twilight Zone* episode and grabbed the watch. She pressed the button again and everything sprang back to life.

Eve grew very fond of that pocket watch. She never particularly liked people, and now she could shut them up entirely for however long she wanted.

She used the watch to stop time for days, weeks, and finally months at a time, enjoying the peacefulness and freedom. One day, she pressed the button and left time paused for nearly 20 years.

She relished the solitude during those two decades. She took whatever she desired. She went to public spots that were always too crowded to enjoy before. She felt so lucky that she could cheat time.

But finally, the day came when Eve missed people.

She figured she'd unfreeze everything for a year, and then go back to living in isolation. She sat in her apartment, looking out the window as she pressed the button on the pocket watch.

The world that had been frozen for 20 years jolted to life.

突然，Eve 想起了劇集《迷離境界》的劇情，然後抓起了懷錶。她再次按下按鈕，一切就回復了生機。

Eve 非常喜歡那隻懷錶。她本來就不是特別喜歡其他人，現在可以讓人們全都閉嘴，而且她可以決定時間長短，太棒了。

她試著用懷錶把時間停止幾天、幾週，甚至幾個月，享受著寧靜和自由。有一天，她按下按鈕，想讓時間停頓了將近二十年。

在這二十年裏，她很享受孤獨。她得到了她想要的一切，也去了以前因為覺得太擁擠，所以沒有去過的公共場所。擁有可以騙過時間的能力，她感到很幸運。

但 Eve 始終還是很想念其他人。

她打算過一年時間正常運作的生活，然後才再次過著與世隔絕的生活。Eve 回到公寓坐下，看向窗外，按下懷錶的按鈕。

被凍結了二十年的世界猛然再次運作。

Eve realized she suddenly felt different; her joints were aching and she was hunching over. She turned towards the nearest mirror and screamed at what she saw. Instead of her 40 year-old face, a frail old woman looked back.

Time had caught up with her.

She dove for the watch and immediately pressed the button again – she didn't want to age another second.

Eve took a hot shower that night, cringing at her wrinkled aching body. She started to step out of the shower when she slipped and fell, slamming her head against the side of the bathtub with a loud crack. She lay there, feeling a warm puddle of blood ooze around her.

As the world started to slip away, she had one thought: *who's going to start the watch up again?*

Eve 感覺到她突然有點不同了，她彎腰時關節會隱隱作痛。她轉向最近的鏡子，因看到鏡中的畫面而尖叫著。本應是一張四十歲的臉，現在換來了一個虛弱老太太的模樣。

時間還是追上了她。

Eve 馬上找來了懷錶，並立即再次按下按鈕——她不想再多衰老一秒。

那天晚上，Eve 洗了個熱水澡，望著自己滿布皺紋又疼痛的身體，感到十分難堪。她走出淋浴間時滑倒了，頭部轟的一聲撞向浴缸的一側。她只躺在那兒，感覺到有一灘溫暖的血液正在滲出來。

隨著世界逐漸消失，Eve 的腦海只得一個想法：*有沒有誰可以把懷錶重新啟動呢？*

While, not For

It's my last day. Retirement! Freedom! The long slog of forty years has finally passed. The cycle of wake, work, eat, sleep will finally be broken.

Starting tomorrow I will finally understand what it is to experience this life. To live out all the dreams I kept inside during my corporate prison sentence.

It's my last hour. At this point I'm practically finished with my working life. Now I just have to get my desk in order, fill out some paperwork for HR and make sure all the loose ends of work are tied up in neat little bows.

Tomorrow I'll be in bed. I'll let my alarm wake me up at the normal time. I'll realize that I'm free. I'll think about all those poor saps who are still working. I'll take the clock and arc it into the wastebasket on the other side of my bedroom. Then I'll lie back in bed to the sweet sleep of morning light.

It's my last minute. I sign my time. I close out the windows on my computer.

When I get home, I'll take the wife to a fancy dinner. We'll go see a movie. We'll stay out late and have a drink.

榮休之喜

今天是我退休前最後一個工作日！長達四十年的艱苦跋涉總算來到了終點，終於可以打破每天「起床，上班，吃飯，睡覺」的乏味循環了。

從明天開始，我終於可以真正享受生活，一直在牢獄般環境下工作的我，終於可以實現夢想了！

來到最後一小時，這個時刻我的工作生涯可以稱得上是完滿結束。現在我只需整理一下辦公桌，填些文件給人事部，確保所有瑣碎的文件都整齊地用小蝴蝶結綁好，那就行了。

明天的我將會躺在床上，讓鬧鐘在平時該起床的時間吵醒自己；讓自己意識到已經不用再上班了，已經自由了；我會想起那些還要上班的可憐蟲；我會把鬧鐘拋到睡房另一端的廢紙簍裏；然後躺回床上，浴在早上的陽光之中再做個酣夢。

來到最後一分鐘，我準備簽名登記離開，關閉電腦裏頭的所有視窗。

當我回到家，我要帶妻子吃一頓豐盛的晚餐，去戲院看電影，還要去喝點東西，待到很晚才回家。

The boss is on his way to wish me well. Previous thoughts of flipping off the boss and laughing as I leave melt away as I exchange pleasantries and shake his hand. He's telling me how the company appreciates my hard work and dedication. How my contributions will be missed. He's wishing me well for my future.

It's my last second. The boss's voice skips. The fluorescent lights flicker. The world freezes.

A voice from the fabric of space declares *"Work cycle complete. Commencing initialization."* My vision turns to static as the office around me dissolves pixel by pixel.

My eyes still wide open take in the view that is revealed. My head moves sluggishly contained within a sticky wet helmet. I look around and see other forms hanging still in the thick turquoise gel. Each head is capped with a thick twisting cable that extends up out of sight. Below the dangling feet lies a nothingness that grows ever darker.

I try to reach for the tether that's holding me up, but my muscles are too weak to move. I look into the faces of those figures facing me. Their eyes are open, but their perception is shut.

看著正要跟我道別的老闆，本想在離職時辱罵他一番，然後笑著離去的我，最後只是彬彬有禮地跟他握手寒暄。他告訴我公司很欣賞我的辛勤工作和奉獻精神，也會很想念我，又祝福我前程錦繡。

來到最後一秒，老闆的聲音突然斷斷續續的，燈光開始閃爍，世界像停頓了般。

一把像是來自外太空的聲音鑽進耳際：「*工作週期完成。開始進行初始化。*」我的視野突然靜止不動，看著辦公室正在逐格消失。

在這般情況下，我的眼睛仍然一眨不眨地睜大了。我的頭在一個黏答答又濕漉漉的頭盔裏緩慢地移動。我環顧四周，看到其他人被包覆在厚重的藍綠色凝膠中。每個人的頭部都有一根粗大的電纜，延伸到看不到的地方。懸垂的腳下面是一片甚麼也沒有、只得黑暗的虛無。

我試著伸手去抓那吊著我的繫繩，但我的肌肉乏力，無法移動。我觀察著那些面向我的人，他們的眼睛是張開的，可是他們沒有知覺。

Then I notice a pair of eyes that are awake. The figure blinks frantically trying to tell me something. Then the eyes slowly return to center and glaze over.

The voice in my head returns to declare "*Initialization complete. Commencing work cycle.*" **A new image begins to form pixel by pixel.**

The alarm goes off. Clawing at my head I fall onto the floor. What was that place? Where am I? The memory of the hanging figures begins to fade pixel by pixel.

I better get ready quick, I need to make a good first impression!

然後我注意到其中一個有意識的人，他不斷眨眼，試圖告訴我某些事情，接下來他的眼球慢慢看回中間，目光變得呆滯。

我腦袋中的聲音又再響起：「*初始化完成。開始工作週期。*」接著，新的影像便開始逐格浮現。

鬧鐘響起。我摔倒在地上，不禁抓抓頭，這裏是甚麼地方？我在哪裡？記憶中的影像逐漸消失。

我要快點做好準備，要給別人留下良好的第一印象！

There's No Reason to Be Afraid

When my sister Betsy and I were kids, our family lived for awhile in a charming old farmhouse.

We loved exploring its dusty corners and climbing the apple tree in the backyard. But our favorite thing was the ghost.

We called her Mother, because she seemed so kind and nurturing.

Some mornings Betsy and I would wake up, and on each of our nightstands, **we'd find a cup that hadn't been there the night before.** Mother had left them there, worried that we'd get thirsty during the night. She just wanted to take care of us.

Among the house's original furnishings was an antique wooden chair, which we kept against the back wall of the living room.

Whenever we were preoccupied, watching TV or playing a game, Mother would inch that chair forward, across the room, toward us. **Sometimes she'd manage to move it all the way to the center of the room.**

We always felt sad putting it back against the wall. Mother just wanted to be near us.

善良的鬼魂

當我和妹妹 Betsy 還是小孩時，我們一家曾經在一間迷人的古老農舍裏住了一段時間。

我和妹妹喜歡走到農舍那些塵土飛揚的角落探險，又會跑到後院爬上蘋果樹。但我們最喜歡的東西是鬼魂。

我們稱她為「母親」，因為她感覺很善良，也很照顧我們。

有些時候，我和 Betsy 在早上醒來時，會發現我們兩個的床頭櫃上，**會突然出現前一晚明明不在的杯子**。這是因為母親擔心我們在夜裏會口渴，所以把杯子放在那裏。她只是想照顧我們嘛。

在眾多農舍主人留下來的家具中，有一張古色古香的木椅，我們把它放了在客廳，椅背靠著後面的牆壁。

每當我和妹妹在全神貫注地做事情，例如看電視或玩遊戲時，母親都會把那張椅子向前推，穿過客廳，向我們的方向推過來。**有時她會設法將椅子移到客廳的中央。**

我和妹妹把椅子放回牆邊時，總是會替她感到難過。母親只是想靠近我們嘛。

Years later, long after we'd moved out, I found an old newspaper article about the farmhouse's original occupant, a widow. She'd murdered her two children by giving them each a cup of poisoned milk before bed. Then she'd hanged herself.

The article included a photo of the farmhouse's living room, with a woman's body hanging from a beam. Beneath her, knocked over, was that old wooden chair, placed exactly in the center of the room.

在我們搬走了很多年之後,我在一份舊報紙上看到一篇關於農舍主人的新聞報道。她是一名寡婦,她在兩個孩子睡前,給了他們每人一杯有毒的牛奶,毒殺了他們,之後她就上吊自殺了。

那篇報道還刊登了農舍客廳的照片,上面有一個懸掛在橫樑上的女人。在她的下方,弄翻了的,是那張古舊木椅,正是放了在客廳的中央。

Regrets

Being stuck in a time loop gives you plenty of time to think about your regrets.

I regret wearing this itchy, too-tight bra. And real pants, I hate those.

I regret not stopping for lunch. In fact, I regret my whole stupid diet.

I regret my choice of music. Drake is great, until you hear the same fifteen seconds on repeat.

I regret forgetting to take my meds. This migraine was brutal and hit so quickly.

I regret driving in the southbound lane in the afternoon. The sun hitting my eyes is a pain. Literally.

But, as the car clears the overpass and I see the cinder block hurtling towards the driver's-side windshield for the hundredth, no, thousandth, time--

...what I regret most is letting my daughter take the wheel.

後悔

陷入了時間輪迴的困境後，讓我有非常充裕的時間反思自己過去的犯下的錯誤。

我後悔穿了這件令我發癢又太緊的內衣，還有這條一點也不舒適的褲子，我實在不喜歡它們，我早該選擇平常在穿的彈性運動褲。

我後悔沒有停下來吃午飯，說實話，我是在後悔一直以來都節食。

我後悔今天的選曲。Drake 的歌很好聽，可是不斷重複聽其中的十五秒就不再動聽了。

我後悔忘記吃藥，偏頭痛來得又快又狠，痛死我了。

我後悔在烈日當空的下午駛入南行車道，太陽把我的眼睛曬得刺痛。

不過當車子駛過天橋，我第一百……不，第一千次看著那塊煤渣磚塊正向司機位的擋風玻璃飛去時，我總是會想起，最讓我後悔的……**是讓女兒開車。**

Breaking Amy

Freddy wasn't your typical 13-year-old. He was an asshole. If he wasn't in his bedroom screaming at video games, he was scaring his 7-year-old sister.

Every traumatizing prank he pulled on little Amy would be worse than the last. Once he had even told her that their mother had been murdered and covered the kitchen floor with ketchup for maximum effect.He was the reason she was so unstable.

She would often tell their mother that she heard whispers and had even seen ghosts wander the house at night. Freddy would giggle at that, almost proud of the damage he had done. But unfortunately for Amy, it was never enough for him. He felt compelled to break her... completely.

The storm had kept Freddy awake that night. Restlessly, he tossed and turned in boredom. For a while he tried to count sheep, but even that didn't help. In defeat, he laid mindlessly watching the raindrops slide down his window.

Lightning flashed suddenly, illuminating his entire room. It was soon followed by a deafening boom. Freddy smiled. He knew what was then to come.

壞心的哥哥

Freddy 不是你想像中那些典型的十三歲小伙子，他是個大混蛋。要是他不在睡房裏邊玩著電子遊戲邊大喊大叫，他就是在嚇唬七歲的妹妹。

Freddy 所做的惡作劇，對年紀那麼小的 Amy 來說，每次造成的創傷都比上一次更深。甚至有一次，Freddy 告訴 Amy 媽媽被殺了，為了使惡作劇更逼真，他更用番茄醬塗滿全個廚房的地板，讓 Amy 嚇破了膽。Freddy 正是 Amy 如此情緒化的元兇。

Amy 常常跟媽媽說聽到有人在她耳邊說話，夜裏甚至看到鬼魂在屋內徘徊。Freddy 每次聽見都會暗地嘲笑妹妹，幾乎為自己對妹妹所造成的心理陰影感到驕傲。可是 Amy 真不幸，因為哥哥都永遠不滿足，他覺得有必要徹底嚇壞她。

那天晚上，一場雷雨使 Freddy 睡不著。焦躁不安的他輾轉反側，躺在床上只感到無聊。有一段時間他試圖數綿羊，可是也無濟於事。感到挫敗的他，漫不經心地看著雨滴在窗戶滑落。

閃電突然閃過，照亮了整個房間，緊接著是震耳欲聾的轟隆雷聲。Freddy 微笑了起來，因為他知道接下來將會發生甚麼事。

Freddy heard his sister crying through the wall, closely followed by a faint pitter patter as she ran to their mother's bedroom. This was it... his moment of fun.

He crept down the hallway and into Amy's bedroom. He prowled around her room like a serial killer, studying every inch of it. Countless ideas rushed through his mind... then he saw the closet.

Freddy waited in the dark for what seemed like forever, peering through a small gap between the closet doors. He had decided that when his sister returned and settled into bed he would begin to whisper. Then, once she was completely terrified he would burst out and run at her, screaming at the top of his lungs.

He had almost lost all hope and was about to leave when he heard the footsteps approaching. His mother opened the bedroom door and Amy slowly shuffled in. She was sucking her thumb and dragging her favourite blanket behind her. As she crawled into bed Freddy couldn't help but grin in excitement.

Freddy watched in silence as their mother tucked Amy tightly into bed, plant a big kiss on her forehead, and finally said goodnight. He waited anxiously until he heard his mother's

Freddy 聽見隔壁房傳來妹妹的哭聲，然後是她跑到媽媽睡房時發出微弱的、啪嗒啪嗒的腳步聲。是時候了⋯⋯是他該搞蛋的時刻了。

他躡手躡腳地沿著走廊走進 Amy 的睡房。他在妹妹的房間裏悄悄地走來走去，研究房間裏的每一吋事物，像極了一個連環殺手。Freddy 的腦海浮現了無數個壞念頭，然後他看到了壁櫥。

Freddy 在黑暗中等了很久，久得像永遠一樣漫長。等待期間，他只凝視著兩道壁櫃門之間的那個小縫隙。他決定好了，當妹妹回到房間，躺回床上的時候，他就會開始低語。然後，當她嚇壞了的同時，他就會衝出壁櫥跑向她，並對她撕心裂肺地尖叫著。

當心灰意冷的 Freddy 打算放棄嚇唬計劃、正想離開之際，他便聽見逐漸靠近的腳步聲。媽媽打開了睡房的門，Amy 拖著腳地慢慢走進來。她正吮著拇指，另一隻手把她最喜歡的毯子拖在身後。當 Amy 爬回床上時，Freddy 忍不住興奮地咧嘴笑了起來。

Freddy 一聲不發地看著媽媽給 Amy 掖好被子，並在她額頭上留了一個大大的吻，最後說了晚安。心急如焚的他，聽見

door close before beginning. This is it. He thought, shaking in delirium. The moment I break her.

"Amy..." Freddy whispered hauntingly.
She didn't respond.

"Amy…" He continued.
Still no response.

"I'm in the closet Amy... come play with me..." He harshly croaked.
"Not tonight **Lucy.**" Amy calmly replied.

Freddy frowned in confusion. She must be sleep talking.

"Wake up Amy… it's not-"

A hand reached out from behind him. It pulled Freddy back into the darkness and clutched over his mouth with a cold tight grip.

"She said not tonight..."

媽媽離去的關門聲便迫不及待地「發功」了。是時候了。他心裏不斷如此想著，甚至亢奮得顫抖起來。是時候使她徹底崩潰了。

「Amy……」Freddy 用怪異的低聲說道。
Amy 沒有回應。

「Amy……」他繼續低聲叫喊著。
還是沒有回應。

「Amy，我在壁櫥裏……和我一起玩吧……」他把聲線壓得低沉嘶啞地說道。
「今晚不玩了啊，Lucy。」Amy 冷靜地回答道。

Freddy 困惑地皺著眉頭。她一定是在說夢話吧。

「醒來吧 Amy……不是──」

Freddy 身後突然伸出了一隻冰冷的手，緊緊摀住了他的嘴巴，並把他拉回黑暗之中。

「她說了今晚不玩……」

Where Were You When Time Froze?

John was at his desk typing away. His keyboard seem to solidify and become as hard as granite. He tried to back away from his desk, but the chair was held rigidly in place. He had to lift himself up and climb onto his desk to get free.

The office was in a panic. Janis was trapped under a blanket and was screaming for help. Several coworkers were attempting to pull the blanket off of her to no avail.

John went back to his desk to retrieve his phone. It too would not budge and he could not unlock it because the power button was stuck. Luckily his keys and wallet were in his pocket and seemed free of this paralyzing curse.

He ran to the central elevator and found one of them was stuck open. Two people were inside frantically trying to get the elevator to move. His next option was the stairwells.

Most of the doors were closed and wouldn't budge, but finally he found one that was open. There were screams from the floor above. He climbed up the stairs in an attempt to help, but the door there was also immovable. Apologizing, he descended the stairs to the ground level. The doors were all closed. There was no way out.

時間靜止當刻你在幹甚麼？

John 本來正在辦公桌上打字，突然鍵盤像凝固了般，變得像花崗岩般堅硬。他想離開辦公桌範圍，可是椅子根本不動如山，於是他只好站起來，跨過桌子逃脫。

整個辦公室陷入一片慌亂——Janis 被困在毯子下，正在高聲呼救，幾個同事嘗試幫她把毯子拉開，可惜徒勞無功。

John 走回他的位置，想拿回電話，然而電話亦一樣紋絲不動，加上電源按鈕卡住了，無法解鎖。慶幸的是，他的鑰匙和錢包都在褲袋裏，似乎沒有被這個「不動咒」影響。

John 跑到外面，打算乘中央電梯，看到其中一部電梯關不了門，電梯裏的兩人發瘋似的想令電梯正常運作。放棄了電梯後，John 只好走樓梯。

大部分的門也緊閉著，一動不動的，最後竟找到一扇開著的門。尖叫聲從樓上傳來，他走到上一層，想幫他們一把，可是那扇門同樣無法移動。向被困的人表示抱歉後，John 走下樓梯，向地面進發。但所有門都關上了，沒有出路。

Trent was in his car. He was talking to his wife on the phone as he was stopped at an intersection. **The cars on the main road ahead of him all suddenly stopped in place.**

The occupants were thrown violently forward while the seat belts held them firmly. No airbags went off and no horns were honking. It appeared as if most of them had been killed or severely injured.

There was confusion on the other end of the line as his wife informed him that something was going on and she had to go. Trent tried to unbuckle and open his door to get out but neither would budge.

He was strapped in place watching the dead and dying. His only consolation was that he was able to talk to his wife again.

Jennifer was out in a field with her husband and kids. They were playing a game when she felt a sharp pain in the soles of her feet. Her children began screaming and crying. Her feet were bleeding profusely and she reached down to feel the grass.

It was impossibly stiff and sharp as razors. Her husband was trying to reach the kids, but the grass tore at his feet with every step.

Trent 當時在車子裏，停在十字路口跟妻子聊電話。**那些在主道路的車，突然全部在他面前停了下來。**

雖然車內的人都有綁上安全帶，卻因為急停的猛烈衝力而受傷。安全氣囊沒有打開，也沒有一聲響號。大部分人看起來似都死掉了；沒死的也身受重傷。

電話另一邊的妻子告訴 Trent 有些事情發生了，所以她要掛線，可是 Trent 卻很困惑。他嘗試解開安全帶並打開車門，但沒有一樣東西可以動得了。

他正被綁在車子裏，眼巴巴的看著別人死掉，也眼巴巴的看著自己快將死去。Trent 只想能跟妻子多説一次話，那就心滿意足了。

Jennifer 正在田野裏跟丈夫和孩子們玩耍，玩得興高采烈之際，她的腳底突然傳來一陣劇痛。孩子們開始尖叫並大哭起來，Jennifer 的腿血流如柱，她彎下身子，摸了一下地上的青草。

那些青草出奇地僵硬，而且像剃刀般鋒利。她的丈夫想走到孩子身邊，可是他每走一步，那些青草都會狠狠剌進他的腳。

Once they reached the kids, they picked them up and started heading for their car in the distant parking lot. By the time they reached the pavement, Jennifer and her husband were dragging themselves along the ground to reach safety. They were able to get the kids to the curb before bleeding out.

I've been stuck in my dorm room, but at least I have my phone available. How is everyone else doing out there? Where were you when time froze?

他們甫走到孩子那邊，便把孩子抱起，然後走向遠處的停車場，找回他們的車子。他們幾經辛苦，終於趕及在失血過多之前，將孩子安全帶到行人路上。

我則被困在宿舍房間裏，但幸好我的電話還能用。外面的你們還好嗎？時間靜止當刻你在幹甚麼？

Get Me Away from Here, I'm Dying

I sit at a wooden dining table, an empty teacup in front of me. My husband sits across from me, staring. **We're not talking. We never do.**

There's only silence. Endless, all-consuming, insufferable silence. I want to scream at everyone, at everything, but I can't. It's torture.

To retain some semblance of sanity, I try to find things to be grateful for. My house is beautiful, one that most people would envy. It's a grand mansion, richly furnished and free of clutter. My clothes are lavish too; I wear a light blue floor-length gown and my husband sports a crisp suit.

But I'm sick of looking at my furnishings, at his suit. I would give it all up for freedom. I want to leave here more than anything, to escape and never look back. I never want to see this house again.

My husband doesn't know this, of course. I have a daughter and son too, **but I never see them.** They're always in their rooms.

My husband smiles at me. I smile back.

厭倦了乏味的生活

我坐在木餐桌前，面前有隻空杯子。丈夫坐在對面，一言不發地盯著我。**我們不說話，從來也不說。**

這裏只有一片死寂——無止境、吞噬一切、令人難以忍受的死寂。我想對所有人或是所有事物都大喊大叫起來，但我不能。這與酷刑無異。

為了保持僅餘的理智，我試著找尋一些值得感恩的事物。例如我的房子很漂亮，漂亮得大多數人都會表示羨慕。這是一間宏偉的豪宅，裝飾華麗，一點也不雜亂。我的衣服也很闊氣——我穿著一襲淺藍色的禮服長裙，而我丈夫也是西裝筆挺的。

但我不想再看著家具和他的西裝了，我很厭倦了。我願意放棄這一切來換取自由。我想離開這裡，沒有甚麼東西比這個想法更重要了，我一心只想逃離，而且永遠不要回頭。我再也不想看到這所房子了。

丈夫當然不知道我這樣想。我還有一對子女，**但我從未見過他們**，他們總是在自己的房間裏。

丈夫對我微笑。我也向他報以微笑。

Inside my head, I'm screaming, wailing, pleading. Get me out of here, please. I'll do anything. Anything to break the silence, the monotony.

As if someone has instantly answered my quiet pleas, the window I'm facing is suddenly obscured as something enormous covers it.

No, it can't be.

Loud noises erupt around me and the ground starts shaking violently. I can't believe it. I thought they were gone for good. I haven't seen them in so long.

A giant eye appears in the window.

"It's still in pretty good shape. Maybe we should hold onto it," a voice booms.

"Honey, please," a deeper voice says. *"We need to get rid of some stuff. The kids haven't used it in ten years. It goes."*

Before I know what's happening, my entire house is being lifted into the air, rising higher and higher. To my horror, it tilts sideways and begins to fall, crashing loudly to the ground. My husband and furniture go flying in every direction.

我在腦海裏不斷尖叫、哀號、懇求著：「請讓我離開這裏。我願意付出一切代價，只要可以打破這個沉默又乏味的生活就可以了。」

好像有人立刻聽到了我心底的請求般，我面前的窗口突然被某些巨大的東西覆蓋著，變得模糊不清。

不，不可能的。

周圍響起了大聲的噪音，地面也開始劇烈搖晃。簡直是難以置信！我以為他們已經一去不返了。好久沒見過他們了。

有隻巨型的眼睛望進我們的窗戶。

*「可是還是保持得好端端的啊，或者我們應該把它留下來嘛？」*一道聲音轟入耳道。

*「親愛的，拜託了。」*另一把較深沉的聲音説道：*「我們要捨棄一些無謂的東西啊，孩子們十年都沒有碰過它們了吧，不要留戀過去了好嗎？」*

在我意識到發生甚麼事之前，整個房子都被抬升到空中，而且愈來愈高。令我驚恐的是，房子傾斜起來並開始向下墮，

"Damn! Dropped it," the deep voice says. *"Ah well, it was trash anyway."*

I'm lying on a wooden floor. I look at my house and family scattered in pieces around me.

I didn't necessarily want this to be what broke the unbearable tedium, but I guess I'll take it. I stare wide-eyed as an enormous foot comes rushing towards me from above. I know what it means, but I don't care.

Because I'm free. I'm finally free.

轟然撞向地面。丈夫和家具全部各散東西。

「*靠！不小心掉了。*」那把深沉的聲音說道：「*啊沒關係吧，反正它只是垃圾。*」

我躺在木地板上，眼巴巴地看著整棟房子和家人散落在自己身邊。

雖然我期待了很久，但我沒有想過竟然會是以這樣的形式，來打破一直以來難熬又乏味的生活。不過我想我還是會接受的。當一隻巨大的腳從上方向我襲來時，我瞪大眼睛。我知道這意味著甚麼，但我不在乎。

因為我自由了，我終於自由了。

Wish Upon a Star

"You gotta be kidding me."

My shovel hit dirt once more, and paused. "Is God even considering the ramifications of entertaining this request?"

"Oh, you know how he is," grumbled my colleague, who was likewise winded. "He likes getting toasted and mass approving wishes for no reason at all. Remember World War 2?"

"Hah! That was a good one. How do you misinterpret "I'd kill for some juice" to be "I'd kill all the jews"?"

"In fairness, they sound quite similar. At least he rectified it afterwards, or Corporate would go down on his ass. Drinking on the job and whatnot."

We pulled the box from the dirt and **emptied out its contents.** I checked the directions towards the house of the recipient.

"Says here we have a six minute window to catch the next shooting star back."

My colleague nodded. "Make sure the address is right. Don't want no poor shmuck getting this all over their carpets."

向流星許願

「你只是在開玩笑吧？」

我把鏟子又再塞進泥土裏，然後停止了動作。「你說啊，上帝有沒有考慮過，答應實現這個願望的後果啊？」

「噢，你應該很清楚祂是個怎樣的人吧。」同事跟我一樣氣喘吁吁地抱怨道：「祂喜歡在沒有任何理由的情況下舉杯祝酒，以及大規模地接納超多的願望。還記得第二次世界大戰嗎？」

「哈！説得真好呢！你覺得正常人會把『我會殺死那些壞人』曲解成『我會殺死全部猶太人』嗎？」

「公平點説，這兩句聽起來真的很像嘛。不過還好祂後來糾正了這個錯誤，不然上層的人會以『在辦工時間喝酒』諸如此類的罪名，把祂打得屁股開花吧。」

我們從泥土裏取出了箱子，然後**把裏面的東西都拿了出來**。我查看了前往收件人地址的路線。

「我們現在有六分鐘的空檔可以追回下一顆流星。」

同事點點頭道：「請確保地址正確無誤。我不想弄錯後，把

"No, no, it's definitely correct. Little Judy Harrows from Alactaser. Her house is right at the edge of town, you can't miss it."

Some people wish for riches, and get an unexpected windfall from the lottery. Others wish for health, and find old ailments clearing up. We aren't nanka; we don't attach ominous footnotes behind every wish. It is true, though, that the owners behind the most innocent of wishes are often the ones who hold the greatest pain.

"Ready?"

My partner hauled the bag up and over his shoulders as I shook my head at God's drunken approval of this wish.

"I want my daddy back."

Not even God can bring back the dead.

But we do what we can.

那些無辜可憐蟲的地毯弄得一塌糊塗啊。」

「不會，不會，絕對正確。這裏寫著是來自 Alactaser 的 Judy Harrows 小妹妹。她的房子就在城鎮的邊緣，一定能 找到的。」

有些人許願希望獲得財富，就會因買彩票中獎，得到一筆意 外收穫的橫財。有些人希望身體健康，那些小病小痛就會不 藥而癒。我們不是邪惡的精靈，我們不會在完成願望後，還 附贈一些不祥的小插曲。然而，確實，許下最天真無邪願望 的人，往往須經歷過最痛苦的折磨。

「準備好了嗎？」

同事把袋子拉到肩膀上的同時，我想起上帝因喝醉了而答應 實現這個願望，慨嘆地搖了搖頭。

「我想爸爸回來。」

即使是上帝，也不能把死者復活。

但我們會盡最大努力，做我們做到的事吧。

To Be Young and Healthy Again

Eugene sat on a bench in a sunny park, watching the vibrant young people bustling around him. They were all office workers who were escaping on their lunch breaks to enjoy the day. Eugene, having just turned 77 years-old and thus retired a decade ago, missed working and having a purpose. He never married or had kids. His friends passed away. He didn't have much to do except sit and watch the foolish people who took their youth for granted. **All Eugene wanted was to go back and do it all over again.**

He had been watching Liam for months now, an attractive 20-something professional who always seemed to be surrounded by friends and lovely women. Years ago, an entity had granted Eugene one wish of his choosing. He had been holding onto it, scared to wish for the wrong thing. It was finally time to use it.

"I wish to trade places with that fellow over there," Eugene whispered softly. "Let me be young again."

He could hardly wait. No more aching joints. No more envying youth. No more boredom.

The next morning, he awoke feeling euphoric. He was in a trendy apartment with expensive furniture. Smiling photos lined the wall. He found a mirror and stared at his attractive

青春常駐，身體健康

一個陽光普照的下午，Eugene 坐在公園的長椅上，看著周圍滿是精力充沛的年輕人在熙熙攘攘。那些年輕人都是在辦公室工作的，大家都趁著午休時間走出來放鬆一下。Eugene 剛剛過了七十七歲生日，十年前已經退休了，很懷念工作和有目標的人生。他沒有結婚生小孩，朋友們也一一去世了。他沒甚麼事好做，只好坐下來看著這些把青春視為理所當然的愚蠢小伙子。Eugene 一心只是想要回到過去，**重新再活一遍。**

這幾個月以來，Eugene 一直觀察著 Liam。Liam 二十多歲，是個有魅力的專業人士，看起來總是被很多朋友和漂亮女生包圍著。很多年前，Eugene 得到了一個實現願望的機會。他很害怕會後悔許錯願，所以一直未有真正許願。現在終於是時候了。

「我想和那邊的那個人交換，」Eugene 輕聲說道：「讓我再次變得年輕吧。」

Eugene 心急如焚，非常期待。關節不再疼痛了，不用再嫉妒青春了，不會無聊了。

第二天早上，他醒來時興奮不已。他身處一間放有昂貴家具的時尚公寓裏。牆上掛著滿是笑臉的照片。他找到了一面鏡

young reflection. He had gotten his wish. He sobbed wildly with relief.

After a short adjustment period, Eugene decided to visit a doctor for a check-up. Some unsettling symptoms had started to hit him after the change; his skin looked discolored and his stomach ached constantly. He found a business card on the refrigerator and decided to start there.

"What can I do for you today, Liam?" the doctor asked as he entered his office.
"I'd like a check-up,"Eugene answered.

The doctor had a puzzled look on his face. "But you've just had a check-up. And we've discussed your results in great detail. Did you have more questions about your diagnosis?"

"What diagnosis?" Eugene asked, his heart thumping in his chest.

The doctor nodded sadly. "Every patient deals with a prognosis like yours differently. Some need to hear it a few times to believe it. Liam, I'm referring to your stage three pancreatic cancer."

Eugene's abdomen hurt worse than ever.

子，不禁凝視著鏡中這個富魅力又年輕的影像。Eugene 的願望已經實現了。放下了心頭大石的他，瘋狂地抽泣著。

慢慢適應過來後，Eugene 決定到診所檢查一下。身份轉換後，有一些令人不安的症狀開始向他襲來：皮膚看起來好像褪色了，而且胃部也持續疼痛。他在冰箱門上找到了一張名片，便決定到那裏做檢查。

「你今天有甚麼需要呢，Liam？」醫生走進辦公室時問道。「我想做身體檢查。」Eugene 回答道。

醫生臉上掛著疑惑的表情：「可是你不久之前才檢查過啊？我們已經非常詳細地討論過你的報告，你對診斷還有不明白的地方嗎？」

「甚麼診斷？」Eugene 問道，緊張得心臟砰砰直跳。

醫生傷心地點點頭：「每個患者聽見病情的預斷後，跟你的反應都有所不同，有些人要多聽幾次才會相信。Liam，我指的是你的第三期胰臟癌。」

Eugene 的腹部從來未如此疼痛過。

Even though several months had passed, Liam was still recovering from the shock of that morning when he awoke to find himself in the body of a 77 year-old man. However, there was one thing that was helping him to get over it.

He had visited a doctor for a check-up and found that despite the normal effects that come along with aging, he was pretty healthy. His doctor had said enthusiastically: "Keep it up and you'll have another 20 years ahead of you!"

Twenty years. The last doctor he spoke with had grimly told him he had a 3% chance of seeing his 30th birthday. Liam smiled.

"I'm old as fuck," he said, staring at his wrinkled face in the mirror. "But at least I'm healthy."

儘管已經過了幾個月，Liam 仍然未能適應每天早晨醒來時，發現自己變成了一名七十七歲男子的震驚感。然而，有一件事可以幫助他感覺好過一點。

他去過診所做檢查，報告顯示除了有一點正常的老化之外，他還是很健康。醫生熱情地跟他說：「好好保持著，你還有二十年的時間呢！」

二十年。與 Liam 交談的最後一位醫生嚴厲地告訴他，他有百分之三的機會可以過三十歲生日。想到這裏，Liam 微笑了起來。

「我都老成這個鬼樣子了。」他盯著鏡子裏滿臉皺紋的自己說，「但至少我很健康。」

I Have to Live Every Day Twice

I live every day twice.

I have ever since I can remember.

As an infant I thought that everyone got to practice a day and then do it for real, I called it **Pracday** and **Today.**

No one else talked about Pracday, and my parents told me what a good imagination I must have. That changed the Today of 'the episode'

I screamed and screamed and kicked and punched and fought.

"We can't go to Granma's because of the Pracday accident"

We stayed home. My parents shouted at each other. Dad's face never did get impaled.

I still have the Pracday scar though.

After that my parents started talking about doctors and medication and hospitals and, and, and, I stopped talking to anyone about Pracday.

預習生活

我每天都要重複生活兩次。

從我有意識以來，就記得生活一直也是這樣過。

當我還是個幼兒時，我以為每個人都像我一樣一會有一天作預習，然後再真正經歷一天，所以我把它們稱之為「預習天」和「今天」。

可是沒有其他人會說有關預習天的事，父母告訴我，我肯定是想像力太豐富而已。可是有一個今天，發生了一段小插曲，改變了我的想法。

我不斷尖叫，又拳打腳踢。

「你再跟我說預習天的事，我們就不去婆婆家了。」

於是我們待了在家。父母互相指責。爸爸的臉上也沒有了刺傷的痕跡。

但那次預習天弄成的傷疤還留在我身上呢。

那次之後，父母開始說起醫生、藥物和醫院等等。而我……沒有再跟任何人談論過有關預習天的事了。

I'm 40 now.

In their hearts and their eyes, my parents know that Pracday is real. Winning the lottery twice in the first two weeks I legally could was stupid of me. Low profile I reminded myself. After all, I've got the time.

An anonymous trading desk on short term stock trades, and a diary.

That has been my life for the last ten years.

Pracday 03/12/2008 A Tsunami hits Indonesia my stocks suffer horribly.

Today 03/12/2008 I dedicated the day to calling in that my equipment was showing a Tsunami incoming, death count -4000. Bank -$100,000

Those calls did bring officers to my mansion door. 3 days before they were satisfied, and I couldn't trade in geo-stock anymore. Still 4,000 lives.

我現在四十歲了。

在父母的心中和眼中，他們很清楚預習天是真的。在前兩個星期，我才合法地贏得兩次彩票，我真笨呢。我提醒自己要保持低調，畢竟我有的是時間。

到匿名交易櫃台交易短期股票，加上一本日記。

我過去十年的生活正是如此。

預習天 2008 年 12 月 3 日，海嘯襲擊印尼，股票急挫。

今天 2008 年 12 月 3 日，我不斷打電話給不同界別的人，報稱我的設備顯示海嘯正在來臨。死亡人數減少四千人。銀行損失十萬美元。

因為打了那些電話，警察來了找我。他們足足監視了我三天才放過我，而且我再也無法交易相關股票了。可是我還是拯救了四千人的性命。

Pracday 07/09/2010 The deadliest American school shooting in 20 years 28 children dead.

Today 07/09/2010 Short sell NRA shares. Bank +$200,000

What god would allow that twice? I had enough warning to do something, how could god not? Long ago I concluded there is no god, no heaven or hell. Just Pracday and Today.

Pracday 06/08/2014 my girlfriend dumped me after a meal at a fancy restaurant, said I had become cruel.

Today 06/08/2014 Jokes on her. I put the drugs in her purse that morning and walked out of that restaurant. After ordering the most expensive wine on the menu of course.

I have gone back and killed her a few Pracdays. The bitch.

I quit the stock market game after $2 Billion. I can take what I want when I want.

預習天 2010 年 9 月 7 日，二十年來最嚴重的美國校園槍擊事件，二十八名兒童死亡。

今天 2010 年 9 月 7 日，賣空了美國步槍協會股票。銀行進賬二十萬美元。

為甚麼上帝會允許這樣的事情發生兩次？我起碼也會警告一下人們，儘量避免事件發生，上帝怎麼可能不警告他們？所以在很久以前，我已斷定這個世上並沒有上帝，也沒有天堂或地獄。只有預習天和今天。

預習天 2014 年 8 月 6 日，和女朋友在一家高檔餐館用餐後，她甩了我，原因是我變得很殘忍。

今天 2014 年 8 月 6 日，我跟她開了個玩笑。那天早上我把毒品放在她的手袋裏，然後離開了那家餐館。離開前當然不忘點了菜單上最貴的酒。

之後的幾個預習天，我都有回去找她然後再把她殺掉。那個臭婆娘。

賺到了二十億美元之後，我退出了股市遊戲。我已經可以隨心所欲地得到自己想要的東西了。

This Pracday: I died. Heart failure.

I Died.

I have never died before, but I guess that's what you get when your heart lives 80 years' worth of days.

They must have called it slightly early because I remember hearing "Time of death 4.05pm"

That... sigh...... that... thing about God. Fuck!

Well I don't know about Heaven. But I spent 9 hours, in Hell. Excruciating. Unbearable. Agony.

This Today:
I position myself in a dedicated emergency room, with the best doctor's money can buy.

3.00pm.

If I survive this, I need to earn my spot in heaven. Or I will have to live everyday in hell, twice.

今天預習天：我死了。心臟衰竭。

我死了。

我之前從來沒有死過，可是我猜，當心臟跳動了八十年後，這也是應得的下場吧。

他們肯定覺得有點早吧，因為我記得曾聽到他們說「死亡時間下午四點四十五分」。

那個，唉，那個……關於上帝的事。他媽的！

呃，我不知道天堂是怎樣的，但我在地獄裏度過了九個小時。非常折磨、難以承受、備受煎熬。

真正的今天：
我自行走到專門的急診室，大灑金錢請來最好的醫生。

下午三點。

如果我活下來，我一定要爭取到天堂的一席位。否則我每天都會在地獄裏，重複生活兩次。

BOOK OF NO 3LEEP

無眠書3

編 譯 解 讀

以下僅為個人理解,並不一定或完全代表作者原意。

別相信任何人

謝謝你,Kelly • 12

致電者是個炸彈狂徒,打電話到報案室假裝求助,讓救援人員進入建築物才引爆炸彈,同時令 Kelly 精神受創。

訊息已刪除 • 16

Anderson 隊長是主角的父親,眼見 Jenna 和主角不歡而散,又得父親撐腰,怒火中燒把他們二人一併殺掉,雖然主角發現了並打算舉報他,可惜證據已被他毀掉了。

Tommy 叔叔的探訪 • 19

Tommy 叔叔懷疑主角被爸爸虐待,於是藉故潛入主角睡房印證事實。

人民慶典 • 22

呼應邪教「人民聖殿教」集體自殺事件,Sadie 的父親極力阻止,最後還是讓母親得逞,Sadie 便因此死去。

姊妹情深 • 24

Tessa 失蹤當時,兇手播放小動物的悲鳴聲,把她誘拐;後來又播放 Tessa 的求救聲,想誘拐 Amy。

她背叛我 • 27

主角綁架了一些孩子,但妻子良心發現,把孩子們救出,並揭發主角的惡行。

清潔工的辛酸 • 29

兇手早有預謀要殺掉太太,而且要主角做代罪羔羊。

我不想知道 • 32

主角殺了兩名女子,其中一位是 Bernadette,而假裝警察的正是 Bernadette 的親友,要向主角報復。

最後一次當保姆 • 34

Lopez 夫婦的家被歹徒入侵,但為了保護小女兒 Denise,便找來當保姆的主角做替死鬼。

他帶我到湖邊 • 37

主角殺了好朋友,所以好朋友弟弟替哥哥報仇雪恨。

雛菊 • 39

主角隨機殺掉一些女孩,但由於他不知道受害者的名字,就以放在墳墓上的花朵稱呼她們。

別理會叢林裏的求救聲 • 41

鎮上的所有人都聽過 Stevie 叔叔編造的故事,害得在叢林迷路的主角弟弟失救而亡。

生人勿近 • 43

主角佯裝成「帶著孩子的媽媽」騙取迷路孩子的信任,然後把他們誘拐回家。

別掉以輕心

相由心生 • 47
主角有看穿別人秘密的能力，不幸地乘上了連環殺手的車子，慘遭毒手。

笑一個吧 • 49
主角不齒那名男子的出軌行為，利用了在動物園工作的優勢，把他餵給獵豹。

神父 • 52
Markus 神父幹了不能見光的壞事，以為無人知曉，卻被上帝揭發，派使神秘男子把神父殺掉。

喝吧喝吧 • 55
汽笛聲代表水開了，Chloe 把滾燙的水餵給 Jess。這想必是每個媽媽的惡夢吧。

牙仙子傳說 • 56
主角一家都視「牙仙子」為傳說，沒想過真有其人，還會強搶小孩的牙齒。

被困黑暗二十年 • 59
可憐的 Pete 因一時笨拙，被困在衣櫥裏死去，二十年後才被恰巧經過的哥哥找回屍首。

長廊的盡頭 • 61
有不明物體入侵了主角的家，她非常害怕，但她更害怕那東西跑到嬰兒室，威脅自己孩兒安危。

警長的聲明 • 63
警長的調查結果顯示，受害兒童不只十三人，而是二十六人，或者更多。

怎樣才算是怪物？ • 66
凡是動物都隱藏著獸性，在極端情況下，人類最好的朋友也迫不得已變成怪物。

流浪貓 • 68
走到地下室的並非流浪貓，而是入侵者，誤闖地下室的 John 發現自己陷入險境，可惜已經太遲了。

黑夜降臨 • 70
呼應「蝙蝠俠父母雙亡」的故事背景，Bruce 為了成為真正的蝙蝠俠，不惜殺害雙親。

色情片被禁以後 • 73
棕髮女生殺掉男朋友後，得知主角正偷窺自己，打算接下來把主角滅口。

別自以為是

悲劇人生 • 78
主角是惡魔，專門在喜氣洋洋的節日出動，展示虛假畫面，讓那些缺乏自信的人都因絕望而輕生。

與十六位惡魔共舞 • 81
主角遇上意外，處於瀕死狀態，體驗了一次另類的人生走馬燈。

假面人 • 85
Becky 不是冒牌貨，主角才是真正瘋掉的人，害死了自己的親生女兒而不自知。

叛徒的餘生 • 88
仁慈的主角不忍心要死囚受苦，卻讓自己成為了首個真正體驗酷刑的人。

長伴身旁 • 91
主角因車禍喪生，但仍然留在女朋友身邊「守護」她。

5070 立方英吋 • 92
主角幸得丈夫相救才不致窒息身亡，不過到底是甚麼讓主角困在小櫃子裏呢？

艾米麗湖的秘密 • 95
妻子說的鬼故事是確實存在的，Emily 的冤魂正在湖中抓她的頭髮，跟她開玩笑。

雙胞胎才懂的事 • 98
主角的哥哥才是連環殺手，主角只是盡雙胞胎弟弟的情義，替他下手。

看門人 • 100
要是不想死後完全沒有存在過的痕跡，我們應要活得精彩，無悔此生。

酒鬼 • 102
妻子的離去使 Martin 染上酗酒惡習，更因酒後駕駛撞死了女兒和小狗，後悔莫及。

無人完美 • 106
以數學算式來解說，「沒有人＝完美」，反之亦然，主角許願希望成為完美的人，結果變成「沒有人」了。

死前七分鐘 • 108
主角企圖自殺後八分鐘便醒覺不想死，可是一氧化碳已對他造成腦創傷，剩餘的七分鐘可能也無法自救。

只得六十秒 • 111
主角只顧留意電視廣播，忽視了染病的妻子，六十秒安全時間即將過去，恐怕他也難逃一劫。

別低估人性

聲軌紋身 • 116
主角和爸爸聯手殺掉媽媽，豈料她死不瞑目，透過紋身向他們討債。

兒童虐待案 • 118
這次的家庭暴力事件，兒子反成了施虐者，虐待主角和丈夫。

槍櫃 • 121
爸爸染病後不斷嘗試輸入密碼，最後成功打開槍櫃，女兒就性命難保了。

我在 Skype 目睹了一切 • 123
主角以為是自己僱用的殺手殺掉不忠的女友，沒想過兇手原來另有其人。

堅定的信心 • 126
主角對 Alice 有堅定的信心，相信她可以了結自己的生命。

紅睡蓮 • 128
紅睡蓮鮮豔的秘密，是因為它吸收了活人的鮮血和靈魂。主角鍾愛紅睡蓮達到病態程度，不惜殺人來種出想要的花。

藏在底下的怪物 • 131
海洋深不可測令人懼怕，但主角的事跡引證：人心遠比遼闊的海洋更可怕。

破釜沉舟 • 134
主角為了贏取巨額獎金，思想變得扭曲，最後更不惜截肢，以達成不合理的減重目標。

抑鬱症治療 • 137
晶片的「療效」正是要令患者自殺，而探員也是受害者之一。

淡黃的一天 • 140
主角因沒出手相救那對小女孩而感到悔疚，每晚也會夢到當天的情境。

指劃女孩 • 143
指劃女孩其實很善良，雖然無法說話，卻一直在旁守護主角，替她躲開了 Banks 先生。

蛇蠍心腸 • 146
主角是死神，與蠍子一起測試人們面對危難時會否捨己救人，從而判定他們進入天堂或地獄。

匯報失蹤人口 • 149
主角被 Tom 拐走並禁錮，但她患上了斯德哥爾摩症候群，反過來同情並幫助加害者，所以警方也救不了她。

別小看世界

罪有應得 • 154
正所謂人在做，天在看，「報應」也有七情六慾，惹怒了它的話，報應來得更狠呢。

永無止境的比賽 • 157
主角和其他人變成了遊戲中的角色，當中的撞擊、觸電、飛墮懸崖等遊戲效果都變成了事實。

惡魔的玩笑 • 159
惡魔根本沒有向主角下詛咒，可是主角因心理影響，讓自己愈來愈倒霉。

生有時，死有時 • 162
Eve 即使得到讓時間停頓的懷錶，最終也是敵不過時間所帶來的痛苦。

榮休之喜 • 165
主角只是一個工作機器，一生只會在拼命工作，不會有退休享樂的一天。

善良的鬼魂 • 168
「母親」並非想照顧主角和妹妹，只是冤魂不散，每天也在重複自殺當天的情境。

後悔 • 170
發生交通意外後，主角不斷重複經歷意外經過，讓她反覆思考最後悔的事，那就是沒有親自駕車。

壞心的哥哥 • 171
Freddy 以為自己把妹妹嚇得有幻覺，但原來真的有些「朋友」會在夜裏跟她玩耍。

**時間靜止當刻
你在幹甚麼？ • 174**
除了人類之外，在時間靜止的瞬間，所有事物都停頓了，你有幸逃脫嗎？

厭倦了乏味的生活 • 177
主角一家都是玩具屋的娃娃，被擱置多年後，主人的爸媽找出玩具屋並把它破壞，主角卻覺得得到解脫了。

向流星許願 • 180
主角和同事是天上派來的使者，負責替人實現願望，Judy 小妹妹想爸爸回來，他們就把爸爸的屍體掘出來放到她家。

青春常駐，身體健康 • 182
主角身在福中不知福，對 Liam 的青春朝思暮想，卻不知道他原來身患重病，命不久矣。相反，雖然 Liam 變成了老伯，但因為有健康的身體，過得非常快樂。

預習生活 • 185
要是主角死後被打進地獄，往後的生活便要接受雙倍痛苦，受盡煎熬。

BOOK OF NO 3LEEP
無眠書3

Contributing Authors
作 者

A. T. White

Heyward Hodges

Brittany Miller

Howard Moxley

Chayan Kumar Bora

J.A. Marshall

Christian Frazier

Juliet Marveaux

Emmanuel Adelabu

Kane Winchester

Gabriel Oro

Kelly Childress

Louise Easter

Seth Bowman
(/u/supersonic3974)

M. Chappel

Tammy Shaw

Nicholas Ong

Tara A. Devlin

Rick Lee

Tristan Lince

Rona Vaselaar

Victoria Mata

Ruby Bones

Viet Dam

Thank you for providing creative and breathtaking stories.
Thank you for making the book enjoyable and relatable.

BOOK OF NO 3LEEP
無眠書3

作者
Author
Short Scary Stories 版區作者
Short Scary Stories Authors

譯者
Translator
陳婉婷
Mia CHAN

出版總監
Publishing Director
余禮禧
Jim YU

特約編輯
Contributing Editor
羅慧詠
Venus LAW

設計助理
Assistant Designer
劉嘉瑤
Sasa LAU

製作
Producer
點子出版
Idea Publication

出版
Publisher
點子出版
Idea Publication

地址
Address
荃灣海盛路 11 號 One MidTown 13 樓 20 室
Unit 20, 13/F, One MidTown,
11 Hoi Shing Road, Tsuen Wan

查詢
Inquiry
info@idea-publication.com

印刷
Printing
美雅印刷製本有限公司
Elegance Printing & Book Binding Co., Ltd.

地址
Address
觀塘榮業街 6 號海濱工業大廈 4 樓 A 室
Block A, 4/F, Hoi Bun Industrial Building,
6 Wing Yip Street, Kwun Tong

查詢
Inquiry
2342 0109

發行
Distributor
泛華發行代理有限公司
Global China Circulation & Distribution Ltd

地址
Address
將軍澳工業邨駿昌街 7 號 2 樓
2/F ,7 Chun Cheong St,
Tseung Kwan O Industrial Estate

查詢
Inquiry
gccd@singtaonewscorp.com

出版日期
Publication Date
2022-2-22（第三版）

國際書碼
ISBN
978-988-79276-7-9

定價
Fixed Price
HKD$98